BATTERED AND BUTTERED WAFFLE

The Diner of the Dead, Book 2

CAROLYN Q. HUNTER

Summer Prescott Books Publishing

**This book is a work of fiction. Any similarities to persons, living or dead, places of business, or situations past or present, is completely unintentional.

PROLOGUE

The television blared in the background, playing a rerun of an old black and white comedy show while Daniel Marston unwrapped his frozen pizza and plopped it in the toaster oven. He only paid partial attention to the television. The episode was one he knew well. A bumbling small-town deputy and his dopey friend snuck into an old, abandoned house to retrieve a lost baseball, and both men were scared witless because they believed the house was haunted.

Haunted indeed, the middle-aged man scoffed with an eye-roll.

Daniel didn't believe in hauntings, but the TV ratings proved that the consumer public thought differently. He worked as an "actor" and writer on a reality show called Ghost Hunters Incorporated, which had been running for the last year. So far, ratings on the show had been insignificant, but he hoped to eventually turn those numbers around. In fact, he was determined to beat out the competition, The Spirit Show, before the year was out.

The Spirit Show was at the top of the rating boards, and the main reason for its success could be attributed to the cast of paranormal investigators, three kids in their mid-twenties who hosted and starred in the show.

From Daniel's perspective, a man in his mid-forties, the three of them were, in fact, kids. It made him furious that a bunch of twenty-something upstarts, kids who did nothing more than wander around with a cheap cameraman in old—supposedly haunted—buildings, were breaking all kinds of television records in a matter of months, records which he himself had only dreamed of. After over twenty years in the wild, weird world of television, and at least ten in reality television, he had little to show for his life's work. Eating frozen pizza in a low-end apartment and watching reruns of old, tired television shows was hardly his idea of a big payoff. Ghost Hunters Incorporated simply hadn't been the cash cow he had hoped for, and after only five episodes the network was considering canceling midseason.

Daniel gritted his teeth just thinking about it, but tried not to worry. He had a plan, something he hoped would give him the huge rating boost he was looking for, and if he was lucky, he'd knock those Spirit kids down a notch. He had a secret weapon that he'd developed that would blow the lid off of the paranormal TV world, and he was waiting for just the right moment to deploy it.

The toaster oven dinged. He opened the oven just as the phone rang.

"What now?" he sighed, heading into the living room where his cell phone was sitting on the couch. It was Carl, his producer. "Hello?"

"Turn on channel 122 right now," Carl instructed, sounding ominous.

"Why?" Daniel asked, picking up the remote and changing the channel. The Spirit Show was on and he groaned in disgust. "Why exactly am I watching this dribble?"

"Just watch," Carl's words sounded like death.

Daniel's eyes, glued impatiently to the screen, widened—first in surprise, and then in anger.

"Now, we'll use The Seer to detect the presence of any entities that might be in the room."

The kid on the screen—the one they called Spirit—pointed toward the device that another cast member, held as though it had magical powers of divination. The device had a flat screen and a cone shaped apparatus attached to the back. Daniel's heart hammered in his chest.

"This device measures when there are changes in airflow or density and then uses cutting-edge technology to outline the disturbance."

The member of the crew, whose public name was "Tech," was holding the device, and he pointed the cone toward a crawl space in the corner of an old house.

"Let's see if we can catch any entities back here," Spirit whispered, moving in close.

The device was Daniel's secret weapon. It was his invention, and it was being used on a rival show.

"What is this?" he barked at Carl. "How were they able to recreate my invention? No one has ever seen it but me, and a handful of people that I trust."

"I have no idea, man. I couldn't believe it when I saw it," his producer sighed.

Daniel paced angrily, his mind whirling. "Where are they filming next?"

"I believe they're doing a few episodes in a middle-ofnowhere town in Colorado called Haunted Falls," Carl replied, reading from a fan site on his computer screen.

"I want to be on the first flight out there."

"No way, man. You can't just go barging in while they're filming. The studio could get sued," the producer protested flatly.

"Fine, I'll make my own arrangements. As of right now, I'm on vacation. I'll call you when I get back," was the terse reply, followed only by the click that ended the call.

Daniel glared at the television screen, at his invention, cursing, and vowed to stop his competitors from using it. He had worked too long and too hard to let Spirit get away with this blatant thievery.

CHAPTER ONE

Sonja's legs felt wobbly as she walked up the stairs and stood on the small wooden platform outside The Waffle, speaking into a microphone.

"Welcome everyone," her voice echoed over the loudspeaker that Vic and Alex had arrived at the diner extra early that morning to set up. "Welcome to the grand opening of The Waffle Diner and Eatery."

A round of applause echoed through the parking lot. At least twenty-five faces looked up at her from the crowd that had gathered in front of the diner, hungry folks from town, all waiting to get into The Waffle for breakfast.

Sonja looked down at Alison, her best friend of almost twenty years and now her business associate. Ally beamed up at her from the sidelines. She stood near the front doors, scissors in hand, ready to cut the ribbon. Alex, Alison's husband, stood nearby with their sweet baby, Cynthia, strapped to his chest. Sonja's mother was also there, clasping her hands in front of her chest, her eyes welling with tears of pride and joy.

"Alison and I are grateful to have you here today. We appreciate all your support as we've worked to get the diner up and running again. We couldn't have done it without your help." Sonja acknowledged a few teenage boys in the crowd who had helped clean up the old diner and get it ready for the grand opening. The boys smiled back.

"But I know you guys didn't come down here just to listen to me talk," she grinned.

"Yeah, we're hungry. Let us in," Sam, one of the boys, shouted, causing a ripple of laughter in the crowd.

Sonja laughed and agreed. "Without further ado, we are now open for business." She gestured to Alison, who cut the strip of red fabric off the front door.

"Let's eat," she announced.

Vic, Alex's father and one of the diner's cooks, pulled open the glass double doors and let the crowd in. The eager diner owner jumped down from the platform and hurried around to the back door, letting herself in and donning an apron. It was time to get things started – with any luck, today would be a long day.

Two hours after opening, the diner was still bustling with customers. Every time one party left, another immediately took their place. It seemed the diner was a hit. Sonja watched gratefully from the kitchen as a few girls from town, whom she'd hired to work as waitresses, bustled up and down between the booths and tables in the dining room—each wearing the signature red and black uniform that she had specifically designed to look vintage, as if the gals had stepped right out of the fifties. Sonja had worked hard to make the interior, as well as the wait staff, appear as authentic as possible, with gleaming chrome and checkerboard floors.

Sonja glanced about the crowded diner, satisfied with how things were turning out. She was more than grateful for the help of her new hires - she didn't think that she, Vic, and Alison could have handled the masses of hungry patrons on their own.

"Another order of gouda waffles, Sonja," one of the servers called from the front.

"On it," she called back. "You gals are doing great out there." The gouda waffles had, to Sonja's surprise, turned out to be quite popular.

The dish was one of the only "gourmet" items she had included on the menu—sort of as an experiment. The new entrepreneur was testing the waters to see if she could successfully fit a diverse selection of dishes on the menu. The residents of Haunted Falls were known for having rather traditional tastes, and "good ol' diner food" seemed to be a staple of small towns. Most customers came in and asked for the usual—a normal plate of flapjacks, or a serving of eggs and bacon, or a stack of waffles. But this morning, it was exciting to see that so many people were willing to branch out and try something new, and as far as she could tell, they were loving it.

She went to work preparing the order. The waffle itself was thinner and crispier than a normal Belgian waffle. Sonja used a crepe style batter, and had a special waffle iron designed specifically to make thinner, crispier waffles. Once the waffle was cooked to perfection, she removed it from the iron and crumbled smoked gouda cheese on top of it. Freshly chopped dates were added on top of the gouda, and the dish was topped off with a warm chocolate drizzle and a dollop of whipped cream. It made for a deliciously sweet, yet savory breakfast item.

Sonja took a second to admire the dish one more time before putting it up in the service window and ringing the bell. "Order up."

"Thanks, Sonja," the server called, grabbing the dish.

Alison came into the back, wiping her brow with the back of her arm. "Whew. It's a mad house out there."

"Aww...it's just a cakewalk back here," Sonja teased.

Her friend grinned. "Okay, okay, yes – I'm grateful that I don't have to stand over a hot stove like you and Vic."

Vic stood at the other end of the kitchen, frying up a fresh batch of hash browns. He laughed and his belly bounced.

"I like the heat," he shrugged, spinning his spatula with a grin.

"Better you than me," Alison replied.

"How is Alex doing with Cyndy?" Sonja asked, pulling another order slip off the turnstile.

"I think he is a little overwhelmed, but he loves that baby girl so much. He'll be fine with her for one day while I help out here."

"Well, we both know he'll put in some serious hours in this kitchen once we're up and running at capacity." Sonja enjoyed feeling like she was part of a true family business.

Vic and Alex, father and son, were brilliant cooks, and she trusted them to whip up whatever whimsical dishes that she invented, in a manner that the Haunted Falls patrons would appreciate. Alison was great with numbers and would be a tremendous help on the business side of things. The young mom also had a special magic when working with customers.

Ally's father had originally owned and run the diner before he passed, and he'd willed the business to his young daughter who had managed the place for a while before shutting it down when the reality of motherhood had taken her by surprise. Alison had been delighted to see Sonja come home from her disappointing "dream job" in New York city, and had convinced her best friend to stay and run the diner. Sonja didn't regret the decision one bit, and hadn't even taken a backward glance when she walked away from New York and her dreams of being a writer. As the new owner of The Waffle, she felt honored to have the acceptance and trust of her best friend and the staff. She'd do everything she could to make the diner successful.

"Anyway," Ally added pensively, "Sometimes I think Cynthia loves her daddy more than me."

Sonja gave her friend a sympathetic smile, thinking that there must be some hormonal fluctuations happening in the new mama. "I'm sure that's not the case, Ally. Cyndy is just used to you being around all the time, she takes it for granted that you'll always be there, and that's not a bad thing. You're her mommy."

"I suppose you're right. I'm really hoping that I get the hang of this parenting thing at some point. It's hard work," she admitted.

"Much harder than running a diner, I'll bet," Sonja nodded. "But at least for now, Alex gets his chance to be with Cynthia all day. I bet it'll make him appreciate what you do at home a little bit more," she grinned, encouraging her friend.

Alison and Alex had agreed to trade off caring for their sweet little Cynthia, and working at the diner. Sonja didn't know how on earth they managed—and couldn't imagine having a child herself—but loved and respected them for it.

"You're right," Ally beamed. "He deserves a chance to be alone with her."

"And a chance to learn about how much work she can actually be," Sonja joked.

Her friend laughed. "He is a really good daddy, actually, completely capable in every way. I think he's probably changed just as many diapers as I have, if not more."

Sonja leaned in and gave her a hug. "You are the luckiest woman I know."

"Well, I'd better get back out there," Ally noted, feeling better. "I don't want to leave my tables waiting."

Moments later, Alison came bursting back into the kitchen.

"Sonja," she hissed, cheeks flushed.

"I thought you had tables waiting?"

"Sonja," she repeated, looking back over her shoulder, her eyes wide.

"What is it?"

Her friend clasped her hands excitedly. "I think a TV crew is here to film the grand opening."

Sonja felt her heart leap. "Really?"

The proud new owner pushed through the swinging double doors that led from the kitchen into the dining area, and looked out the front windows. Sure enough, a large van and a crew of people were unloading film equipment in the parking lot.

"See? It's a film crew."

"You're right," Sonja replied in a hushed voice, unconsciously reaching up to pat her hair.

All of the crew members looked very young, maybe in their early to mid-twenties.

"They look too young to be a professional news crew," she commented, leaning into Alison.

"Well, maybe they're a high school or college film crew."

"Maybe," Sonja frowned, puzzled.

She doubted that a small-town community college or high school news club would have the funding to buy the kind of expensive equipment they were unloading. No, something definitely seemed odd, and a trickle of fear unfurled in the pit of her stomach.

The crew members walked swiftly toward the diner. There were three of them, two men and one woman, followed closely by a slightly older-looking cameraman who had apparently begun filming.

Sonja put on her best "I'm the Boss" face, and came out from behind the counter to greet them.

As they bustled into the diner, one of the young men, with jet-black, slicked-back hair, spoke directly to the camera.

"Hello, ghost hunters. This is Spirit, talking to you directly from The Waffle Diner and Eatery, in the tiny town of Haunted Falls, Colorado. This seemingly innocent small-town diner may look perfectly harmless now, but not too long ago, a gruesome discovery was made in the walk-in freezer, and it wasn't cockroaches, folks...it was a body. Was the victim murdered here? Or for some reason, unknown to anyone of this world, was this just the most hospitable place to hide her earthly remains?"

Sonja felt her stomach turn. Her mouth went dry and acid burned at the back of her throat. This was clearly not a local TV news crew, and they definitely weren't interested in the diner's grand opening.

"The victim, a local, middle-aged woman, was found in the freezer by the current owners, who, for some reason had closed the diner down for a period of time. Coincidence?" Spirit continued, staring intently into the camera, eyebrows raised.

The new hostess who had been busy seating another couple when the crew barged in, ran up to her boss in a tizzy.

"I'm so sorry, Sonja. They just sort of blew past me. I didn't know what to do," she worried.

The entire diner had gone quiet, and customers, friends, and tourists alike were staring at Spirit as he narrated. Sonja felt a small flame of anger flicker within her, but took a deep breath, determined to act professionally. She had hoped to put the recent murder case of Ronda Smith—and the body she and Alison found in the freezer—behind them, so that everyone could focus on the happy news of the grand opening.

Refusing to allow the nonsense to continue, Sonja set her jaw and made a beeline for Spirit.

"Is her ghost still present in this building, seeking solace? Seeking revenge?"

His narrative gave Sonja a sudden chill. The mere mention of ghosts made her hands clammy and her skin cold. She hadn't told anyone about the face that she'd seen in the window after the murder, not even Alison. After that first incident, she had experienced similar supernatural events a few more times during the course of the investigation, but once things had been wrapped up, she'd been left alone by things that go bump in the night, and that's the way that she wanted to keep it. She'd only recently gotten back to being able to sleep with the lights off.

Taking another deep breath, Sonja smoothed out her apron, and regained her composure.

"Excuse me," she called, trying to politely capture Spirit's attention.

"Let's talk to some of the locals and ask them if they've noticed anything strange happening around the diner." The rude ghost hunter never even glanced in her direction, and strode through the eating area like he owned it.

She was being deliberately ignored. Worse than that was the fact that the entire diner was seemingly captivated by Spirit's presentation.

"Can you believe this?" Sonja complained to Alison, her mouth open in astonishment.

"Oh, my gosh," Ally whispered. "I know who they are."

"Who? Who are they?"

"They're the Spirit Crew from The Spirit Show."

"What does that even mean?" Sonja didn't watch much TV and had never heard of Spirit and his crew.

"It's one of those ghost hunting reality shows. They're really popular right now. Alex watches them." Alison pointed at them. "That's Spirit, Tech, and Maddy the Mystic."

That explained it. Many of the customers were probably fans of the show, so they were rightfully amazed to see the Crew walk right into their small town diner in Haunted Falls. The crew moved from table to table, invading the personal space of multiple customers, pushing the camera in their faces while Spirit asked questions. Some customers looked thrilled, others looked horrified. One customer looked as though she might faint when the camera pointed her way. Sonja took off her apron and threw it on the counter.

"I don't really care who they are, they can't be in here right now."

She marched over and tapped the gentleman—Spirit—on the

shoulder. “Hello, Spirit, is it? Can I do something for you?” she raised a warning eyebrow at him.

He spun around to face her. “Ah, you must be one of the folks who work here.” He gestured to the cameraman to get Sonja in the shot. His clearly deliberate “run a hand over my hair to look suave” tactic did nothing for the outraged owner.

“I’m sorry, is your name Spirit?”

He flashed a smile of perfectly white, perfectly straight teeth. “The one and only. We’re interested in the recent murder that took place in Haunted Falls. Do you have any comments on the supernatural incidents that are rumored to be occurring here?”

She bit back the response that leapt to her mind, trying to put her most professional foot forward. “Look, Spirit, I’m going to have to ask you to leave, you can’t film in here.”

The pompous TV host’s smile only widened. “Let me explain. I am Spirit and this,” he gestured to his comrades, “is The Spirit Crew. We investigate potential hauntings and supernatural hotspots and share our adventures with the world on The Spirit Show.”

“Well, if you had bothered to call me ahead of time to try and schedule a time to film, you’d have known that coming out here would be nothing but a waste of my time and yours. In case you hadn't picked up on it, we're having our grand opening right now," Sonja was in no mood to be trifled with by some Hollywood type.

"Do you know anything about the murder that happened here in Haunted Falls?" the host pressed on, completely ignoring her jibe.

"You're done here, Spirit. Take your crew and leave," she insisted, feeling her face begin to flush with anger.

The ghost hunter's eyes grew wide with realization. "You're the owner, aren't you?"

"Yes, I am. My name is Sonja Reed, and I need you to leave now," she said through her teeth, fighting to remain calm.

He turned to the camera.

"Ladies and gentlemen, this is Spirit talking to you directly from The Waffle Diner. We're here right now, talking with the owner of the diner, the very woman who found the dead body only a few weeks ago in her walk-in freezer."

Sonja had had enough. "Let me see...how can I make myself

clear? Oh, I know...get out," she squared off on the obnoxious twit.

"Tell us, Sonja. What was the first thing you felt when you saw the body? Were there any type of energies in the air? Have you yourself seen or felt any supernatural disturbances in the diner since the murder?"

Sonja's face flushed scarlet with rage. That was the final straw - she had no desire to discuss her supernatural experiences with this arrogant young man, or anyone else for that matter. As far as she was concerned, the incidents had never happened – they were a memory shoved back into the far recesses of her mind and she needed them to stay there.

"Get. Out!" her voice rose, sounding a bit hysterical, and she trembled with anger, but jabbed a finger into the young man's chest.

Spirit gazed into her eyes as if he could charm her into doing what he wanted. She was not a violent person, but was more than ready to throw this strapping young man out bodily if she had to.

"Come on, Spirit," Maddy the Mystic interrupted, glancing nervously between the two of them. "She wants us to leave."

His only response was that a corner of his mouth twitched up into an arrogant grin, as he continued to stare at the diner owner.

"Come on, man," the other guy in the trio agreed. "Let's get out of here."

Sonja didn't budge, staring down the ghost hunter with venom in her eyes.

"Look, there's no need for hostility here, just answer one simple question for me," Spirit insisted, with a smarmy grin. "Have you experienced anything supernatural here in the diner?"

"Alison, call the sheriff." Sonja glanced briefly at her astounded friend, who responded with a nod and ran into the diner's back office.

"Are you afraid to answer the question because of things you've seen?"

Sweat appeared in tiny beads on her brow, and her heart thudded anxiously in her chest, giving away the emotional reaction that she had to his intrusive question. For a brief moment it felt almost as if someone...or something, was watching her. Someone other than the predator in front of her was waiting for her response.

"Has your safety been threatened by an otherworldly presence?"

The exasperated diner owner took a deep breath and gritted her teeth, ridding herself of the eerie feeling and regaining her composure.

"My partner is calling the police. If you're not out of her by the time they arrive I'll be forced to press charges for trespassing, disturbing the peace, and impeding commerce."

The host gave her a knowing look and turned back to the camera. "It seems the diner owner herself is too afraid to tell us about the terrifying things that she has seen. Perhaps because she is afraid of the horrors that a murdered ghost might visit upon her."

Sonja began scanning the diner, looking for big, burly men who might be able to help her forcefully eject the overly-dramatic ghost hunter from the diner, when, thankfully, the door to the diner opened and a rugged blond-haired man representing Haunted Hills finest walked in.

"What's going on in here?" Sheriff Thompson demanded, immediately sizing up Spirit and his crew.

Sonja nearly collapsed with relief.

"Thank goodness. Sheriff, these people are trespassing and disturbing the customers. I've asked them repeatedly to leave and they've refused."

The sheriff stepped forward. The cameraman lowered the camera, and Spirit turned on him.

"What are you doing, Benjamin?" he growled. "Keep filming."

"Spirit," the cameraman protested. "Let's just get out of here. We can always come back when it's more convenient for the owner."

"I said keep filming."

"That's just about enough," Sheriff Thompson observed, in a tone that brooked no nonsense.

The entire film crew turned to face him.

"Do you have a permit to film on this location, young man?" he drawled, putting Spirit in his place.

"We're the Spirit Crew," Spirit shrugged, acting like the sheriff should know what that meant, and be impressed by it. "We seek out the supernatural."

"I don't care if you're The Queen of England," the sheriff replied. "You need to either show me a valid permit or I'll be happy to escort you from these premises."

Sonja was taken aback. She had never seen anyone attempt to defy Sheriff Thompson, and was thankful that he was able to react far more coolly than she had under the circumstances.

The female reporter and the cameraman both nodded. "We understand," Maddy said quickly, heading for the door.

"Yes, sir," Benjamin added, lowering the camera and looking embarrassed.

"We're not done," Spirit stood his ground, feet spread apart, arms crossed defiantly over his chest. "We need to get some raw interviews with local citizens."

"Come on, Spirit," Maddy said in a low voice. "We're leaving."

With that, the two crew members and the cameraman hustled out of the diner, leaving Spirit standing alone with Sheriff Thompson.

Spirit muttered like a perturbed child. “Fine. We’ll go ahead and get the stupid permit.”

“Don’t forget,” the officer smiled pleasantly, “you have to have the owner sign it.”

He motioned toward Sonja, “You have to have her permission to film here.”

“We’ll be back,” he smirked and strolled out the door.

“I can’t believe how rude they were,” Sonja muttered angrily, sitting across the table from Sheriff Thompson, sipping her cup of coffee. They were in a small red leather booth in the back corner of the diner.

“It’s show business, I suppose,” he remarked. “That boy’s just a diva.”

“Diva is an understatement,” she snorted. “He is probably the most entitled person I’ve ever met. I would never want to work in television if I had to deal with people like that.”

Alison came over to the table. “You need more coffee?” she asked, holding up the pot.

"No, I should really get back to helping in the kitchen," Sonja sighed, glancing ruefully at her nearly-empty mug.

"You've had a bit of a stressful situation," the sheriff observed. "I think everyone would agree that you deserve a little break."

Sonja leaned over on the table, setting her coffee down. "How did you get here so fast? I mean, Ally went in back to call the station and you walked in the door."

"I didn't even have to call," Ally commented. "He was already here by the time I picked up the phone."

The sheriff smiled. "I was just coming in to eat breakfast, and happened to be in the right place at the right time."

"Well, I'm sure glad that you showed up when you did," Sonja remarked.

She finished off the last of her coffee and stood up. "I really should get back to helping in the kitchen. I don't want to make Vic fill all the orders on his own."

"Alright, then," he nodded. "Can I order before you take off?"

"Hey, how about a meal on the house?" Sonja suggested, more than grateful for his timely intervention. "What would you like to have?"

"What do you recommend?" he asked.

"The gouda waffles are divine," she grinned.

CHAPTER TWO

"You and Frank seem to be getting along nicely," Alison teased, wiggling a finger at her friend, as they stepped back through the kitchen door, after Sonja's short break.

"Who's Frank?" Sonja asked.

Ally put her hands on her hips. "Frank? Frank Thompson?"

Sonja thought for a moment, then her eyes widened with realization.

"You mean Sheriff Thompson?"

A mischievous smile appeared on Alison's face. "I think he likes you."

"Sheesh, Ally," she rolled her eyes. "Isn't he like seven or eight years older than me?"

"What difference does that make?" her friend challenged.

Sonja turned toward the waffle iron and poured in a helping of the crepe batter for Sheriff Thompson's order. "It makes a big difference to me."

"Oh, come on, Sonja. When was the last time you had a date?" Ally stood tapping her foot, hands on hips.

"I don't know and I'm not sure I care," Sonja could feel a heated blush rising from her neck to the tips of her ears.

Honestly, she simply hadn't met anyone she would even consider dating, and even if someone had come along, Sonja thought the whole formality of dating was a painfully awkward process.

"Don't you think Frank—"

"Sheriff Thompson," Sonja corrected. It just didn't seem right calling him Frank.

"Sheriff Thompson. Don't you think Sheriff Thompson is even a little cute?"

"No, I do not," Sonja declared, fully recognizing the lie that came sliding out so quickly. "Besides, I think you should only date people who you're already friends with."

"You and Sheriff Thompson are sort of friends."

Sonja gave her friend a sideways look, opened the waffle iron, and pulled out the finished waffle. "Hand me the gouda, will you?"

Ally grabbed the gouda and handed it to her.

"Thanks."

"Well, you guys seem pretty chummy to me," she persisted, stifling a giggle.

"He thinks I'm a nuisance more than anything else," Sonja chuckled.

"You mean because you got nosy about that murder case?"

Nosy. Sonja really disliked that word. Inquisitive or curious were much more accurate in her opinion.

"I'm not nosy," she defended.

Ally raised her eyebrows and Sonja ignored her.

A tray of dirty dishes appeared in the service window.

"Table five is finished," the waitress called.

"Thanks," Sonja replied, grateful for the interruption of the insufferable conversation that Ally insisted upon having.

"Anyway," Alison sighed, her tone shifting abruptly from playful to serious. "Do you think it was a good idea?" she grabbed the tray of dishes and scraped the leftover food into the trash.

"What do you mean? About Sheriff Thompson?" she asked.

"I mean, telling that film crew to shove off?"

Sonja's jaw dropped. "Why wouldn't I tell them to shove off?"

She was surprised Ally even brought up the film crew again. “I thought you were on board with getting them out of the diner.”

“I was.” She set the dirty dishes in the industrial sized sink to be washed. “But, I’m just saying.”

“Ally, they were incredibly rude. They were disturbing the customers. Would you like to hear about dead bodies and ghosts over breakfast?”

“I guess that depends.”

“Depends on what?”

“Depends on my mood. I’m sure there are lots of people who talk about ghosts over breakfast,” she shrugged.

Sonja grabbed a handful of dates, plopped them on the chopping board, and began cutting them into small chunks. “I don’t care what The Spirit Crew does, or what they think. I care about my customers.”

“Well,” Ally took a breath. “I was just saying. While I agree with you about how rude and disruptive they were—”

"How disruptive he was, you mean. That Spirit character is just like a spoiled child with no manners."

"I can't help but think what it could mean for our future."

"I'm not following what you're trying to say," Sonja's eyes narrowed.

"Well, The Spirit Show is currently one of the top-rated reality shows on television. If The Waffle appeared on that show, we could potentially have a huge spike in business. Fans of the show might travel from all over the country just to see the haunted diner."

Alison's voice warbled as she said, "the haunted diner," waving her fingers in the air like a ghost.

Sonja sighed. She was so blinded by how angry and scared she felt—especially once Spirit brought up ghosts—that she hadn't even considered the idea that national exposure might help increase business at the diner. While she still felt justified in asking them to get a film permit, she wondered if maybe she had overreacted a little.

"I still feel like they were awfully rude," Sonja reiterated, justifying her own reactions to herself. "But maybe you're right. Maybe if they bring a permit for me to sign, I'll give my permission for them to film in the diner."

"It could prove to be very profitable," Alison stated matter-of-factly. "For both of us."

Sonja nodded. "I know."

"Sometimes we have to put our feelings aside for the sake of the business. That's just how it goes."

Sonja smiled faintly. She hated it when her friend was right.

Alison ran the diner for years, even before her father died, and quite a long time before Sonja came on the scene. Now they shared the business—but the young mother had decreed that, ultimately, Sonja was the owner and manager.

Alison had warned her friend that she might not be able to help too often, her first priority was her beautiful new baby, but she'd been at the diner every chance she could, to help out.

"Thanks for your advice."

"No problem. What are friends for?" Ally grinned.

"And for all your help with the diner," she added.

"I'm a creature of habit," Alison declared proudly. "I ran this business—or watched daddy run the business—my entire life. This could be a good boost for us now that the diner has reopened under a new name."

"And under new management," Sonja chuckled. "Management who is having a tough time learning on the job."

"Good thing you're a fast learner," her business partner commented, trying to lift the garbage bag out of the pail.

"Hey, I'll get that. Go ahead and check on your tables."

"Thanks," Ally replied, heading out of the kitchen.

Sonja tied the trash bag and pulled it out of the pail, then stepped outside to place it in the dumpster.

"That woman was such a stick in the mud," she overheard someone saying. "Can you believe how she treated us? What a hag."

Were they talking about her?

Sonja peeked around the corner of the diner and could see the film crew standing near their van in the front parking lot, talking. The cameraman—Sonja thought she remembered his name being Benjamin—was working, loading things back into the van.

She noticed, in spite of herself, the cameraman's bulging muscles as he lifted heavy equipment into the back of the vehicle. She hadn't had the time, or space of mind, to see it before, but he was a tall and ruggedly handsome kind of guy. He was the complete opposite of the fat, balding, middle-aged stereotype often associated with cameramen.

"That woman totally ruined our shot," Spirit complained.

"Well, Spirit. You did barge in on her unexpectedly during business hours," Tech reminded. "And during their grand opening no less." He pointed toward the fabric sign hanging out front.

"Shut up, Tech," Spirit snapped rudely.

"No," Maddy chimed in. "Tech's right. You were really nasty in there. You took it too far this time."

"What do you know?" the perturbed television star turned away from his crew, arms crossed, jaws clamped shut.

"She had every right to kick us out," she responded.

"I told you we needed a permit," Tech added. "But you always want to skip that part. If we want this show to continue to keep its high ratings, we need to make sure we do things right."

"Look, do you guys want to make a good show or not?" Spirit demanded. "Because I'm pretty sure I could carry this show all on my own, without either of you."

"Spirit!" the girl exclaimed, her brow furrowing in an angry warning.

"Whatever," Spirit, exasperated, kicked at some loose gravel in the parking lot. "Maybe we'll have better luck at the old haunted barn."

"Maybe we should get a film permit first."

"No, we're going now," the belligerent host decreed. "Get in the van."

Sonja couldn't believe her ears. Were they thinking about going out and bothering old Mr. Hinkley too? As an old friend of the family, she couldn't stand the thought of it.

"Uh oh, guys," Benjamin warned. A silver sports car pulled into the parking lot and stopped right next to the van.

"What now?" Spirit complained, turning to face the silver car.

The car door opened and a tall man with salt and pepper colored hair erupted from it, looking furious. If he'd been a bull, Sonja could imagine steam erupting from his nostrils.

"Daniel," Spirit smirked. "How good to see you."

"You stole my invention," the man invaded the space bubble of the comparatively small TV host, towering over him.

Not only was he tall, but he looked thick as well. His arms seemed to strain the sleeves of his t-shirt.

Spirit laughed and waved a hand at the older man. "Get out of my face, Daniel. You don't scare me."

Daniel turned so red that he was nearly purple and Sonja was afraid he might have a stroke right there in the parking lot. "You stole my invention, you little sideshow freak. You need to give it to me right now."

"I don't know what you're talking about," Spirit blinked innocently, his mouth twisted into a mocking grin.

Like lighting, Daniel grabbed him by the front of his very expensive shirt, picked him up, and slammed him against the side of the van.

"Hey! Stop it," Maddy shouted, grabbing the large man's arm and pulling. He didn't budge.

"Hey, man. Get off me," Spirit screamed between his teeth, more angry than scared.

Sonja watched, open-mouthed as Benjamin and Tech ganged up on the thickly-muscled man, dragging him away from the 'prima donna' host. Her heart thundered watching Benjamin leap into action. She felt thrilled and nauseated all at the same time. Immediately, she imagined her mother at home, in her armchair by the fireplace, reading one of those "bodice ripper" romance novels. The shirtless man on the front of her mother's most recent novel The Cowboy's Promise came to mind. She wondered what Benjamin might look like on the cover of a book...

Sonja shook her head, trying to clear the steamy daydream from her mind.

"Give me The Seer," Daniel growled, struggling with the two men. "That was my invention."

"I'm not giving you anything. You don't have a monopoly on new ideas," Spirit coolly inspected his manicure, not looking at his outraged competitor.

"That was my project. My invention. And you stole it."

"Look, if you're so certain it belongs to you then go ahead. Sue me. Let's settle it in court...unless you think that you don't have a case." Spirit smiled mischievously.

Daniel's face turned an even deeper shade of red, and Sonja was glad that he was being restrained. She didn't want to see what would happen to Spirit if he got loose.

"What's going on out here?" Sonja heard Sheriff Thompson's voice.

"Oh, thank goodness," she whispered. He must have seen the commotion from inside the diner.

Daniel looked at the sheriff and glared back at Spirit. "This isn't over," he growled, shrugging off the crew that had held him.

"Oh, I think it is," Spirit declared proudly.

The burly man got in his sports car, slammed the door, and drove off, cutting over a patch of dirt and leaving a cloud of dust in his wake.

CHAPTER THREE

Sonja stepped back into the diner wondering what exactly she had just witnessed. If anything, the exchange underscored the certainty she never wanted to work in "show biz." As far as she could tell, those people were all completely nuts. Except for, maybe, Benjamin. The recently enamored diner owner sighed inwardly, her thoughts traveling back to those muscles...

"Where were you?" Alison asked, bringing in more dirty dishes from the dining area.

"Sorry, I got stuck outside."

"Stuck outside? The back door shouldn't be locked."

"It's not," Sonja commented. "But I did just watch a strange fight."

"A fight?" Ally raised her eyebrows. "Who was fighting?"

She recapped everything she saw, but chose not to mention how she had "noticed" Benjamin.

"Daniel? Maybe it was Daniel Marston," Alison guessed.

"Who's Daniel Marston?"

"He is the host of another reality show, Ghost Hunters Incorporated. It is basically a copycat of The Spirit Show, and it certainly isn't doing as well. It's on one of those wanna-be channels."

Sonja shook her head. "How do you know all this stuff?"

"Alex watches a lot of TV at night, so sometimes I sit and watch it with him."

Sonja would never be caught dead watching reality TV, but she certainly didn't judge Ally for it. If that was how she and Alex chose to relax at the end of the day, good for them. She just didn't understand the attraction.

"Well, anyway," Sonja said, "I think someone should run out to Hinkley's farm and warn him that he's about to be invaded."

Alison looked shocked. "Oh my, yes. Hinkley hates visitors as it is. I mean ever since Mrs. Hinkley died, he just sort of keeps to himself."

"I know. That's why I'm worried," Sonja sighed. "If we catch the sheriff before he leaves, maybe he can get out there before Spirit and his crew do, and keep them from bothering Mr. Hinkley."

"Oh," Ally frowned, seeming reluctant, "I don't know if that's a good idea."

"Why not?"

"Well, I just served Sheriff Thompson his food. If he leaves now, it'll get cold, and he's already had to deal with the Spirit Crew once already."

"Twice," Sonja corrected. "He had to break up the fight outside."

"All the more reason," Ally replied. "Why don't you go out there?"

"Me?" she asked. "But I have to stay here at the diner. It's opening day."

"Don't worry. Vic and I will hold down the fort. Won't we, Vic?"

Vic twirled his spatula and nodded without looking away from the eggs he was cooking.

"The Hinkleys have been friends with your mom for as long as I can remember, and he likes you," she reminded Sonja.

"That's true," she admitted.

"So, I think you should go warn him."

"I think you're right," Sonja agreed, finally, unable to argue with Alison's logic.

"But you'd better hurry if you want to beat them to the farm," she prodded.

"Alright," she took off her apron and hung it by the door. "I'll be back as soon as I can."

"Good luck," Ally encouraged with a wave.

The drive to Hinkley's farm was beautiful no matter what the time of year, and today was certainly no different. Sonja crossed the small wooden bridge constructed over a canal, which channeled water runoff from the mountains to the farm and also down to the rest of the town. Once across the bridge, she turned down a narrow dirt road which cut through a grove of vibrant aspen trees. Flowers of all colors popped up all along the road, adding an almost mystical beauty to the grove.

She emerged from the grove into the vista of a wide open field of more reds, yellows, and greens nestled up against the mountain. The road curved around the perimeter of the field and came up past the barn, practically on the doorstep of Mr. Hinkley's farmhouse. Bringing her mom's aged sedan to a halt, she noticed with dismay that the Spirit Crew van was already parked just outside the barn. She swung the car around and pulled up right behind them as they were unloading equipment. Benjamin turned from his work and looked at her. Despite herself, Sonja felt a shiver of excitement, but willed the feeling away.

She opened her door, but before she could say anything, Mr. Hinkley shouted from inside the farmhouse.

"What in tarnation are you hooligans doing out here?" he shouted from behind the screen door.

"Okay, let's roll," Spirit directed his crew, not responding to the old man.

"What are you doing on my farm?" Mr. Hinkley pushed the screen door open. "You got no right to be on my land."

Spirit pushed Benjamin inside the barn.

"He's right," Sonja joined in, appalled. "You have no right to be here without a film permit. Do we really have to go through this again?" she challenged.

The insistent TV host stopped and looked back toward Sonja. "You following me?" he asked, winking at her.

The farm's owner leaned on his cane for support and made his way down the steps. "Who are these people, Sonja?" he asked, his brow furrowed.

"Spirit," Sonja shouted.

Spirit glanced back, surprised to hear her use his name.

"You and your team have no right to be here. This is private property, and you're trespassing."

The young star sighed and turned around to face her. "Look, we're just going to film a few shots and we'll be on our way. Let's all just be chill about this."

Sonja boldly approached him and folded her arms. "No, you're not. It really doesn't matter what you want, you haven't done the proper paperwork to film here."

Spirit shook his head, mocking her. "Don't you people understand who we are? We'll be able to put your little hick town on the map," he sneered.

"We don't want you to," Mr. Hinkley barked, caning his way over. "I don't care who you are or what you're here to do. I've lived in this town since it was a spit, and I'm getting real sick of people like you trying to come in a make a quick buck off us."

"Look, man," Spirit said, rolling his eyes. "We're from a television show."

"I don't care where you're from, you scalawag. You aren't going to just waltz in here and do as you please."

The arrogant young man raised an eyebrow and looked at the farmer like he was from another planet.

"Unbelievable," he muttered under his breath. "Look, if you just give us a few minutes to film..." he began.

"I'm calling in the law if you don't move your buddies, your camera, and your van off my property right now, you young cur," Mr. Hinkley waved his cane in Spirits' direction.

Spirit snickered. "Whoa, slow down old-timer, you don't need to blow a gasket."

"I mean it," Mr. Hinkley stepped forward, and the pompous young man twirled his finger by his ear, signaling the crew to pack it up.

The crew piled their things quickly into the van and zoomed off down the dirt road, leaving a veritable smoke-screen of dust behind them.

Sonja let out a sigh of relief. "I'm sorry about that, Mr. Hinkley."

He looked up at her with a smile. "It's good to see you, little lady. I'm glad you came out."

"I overheard them talking about coming here, and I didn't want them bothering you or disturbing the farm."

"I appreciate it, dear," the old man's eyes twinkled. "I don't know what I would have done without your help."

She laughed. "My help? It seemed like you took care of things pretty easily by yourself."

"All the same. I appreciate it," he turned to climb the steps. "Come in and have a cup of coffee with me?"

"I actually better get back to the diner," Sonja replied ruefully.

"Oh, come on," Mr. Hinkley motioned for her to follow him up the stairs. "I don't often get visitors; let alone visitors that I actually like. Have a cup of coffee with me," he insisted, making the laborious climb.

She didn't have the heart to say no. "Alright, but just for a little while," Sonja agreed following him up the stairs into the farmhouse.

Despite the effort that it was taking him to get up the stairs, the old man smiled and nodded his head. He'd get out the good coffee cups today.

CHAPTER FOUR

Sonja sat and sipped her second cup of coffee that day, relishing the feeling of the caffeine buzzing through her system. That, and the easy-going conversation with an old family friend were just what the doctor ordered.

"Thanks for the coffee," she sighed in contentment.

"Oh, don't be ridiculous, the coffee is sludge," Mr. Hinkley insisted, clearly pleased.

She had to disagree. The coffee tasted pretty darn good in her estimation. "I like it," she told him. "It's raw, simple, and exactly what I needed."

"Well, I'm glad to hear it," with a shaky hand he poured another cup for himself.

“It has a slight nutmeg flavor.”

He snorted. “It’s probably just burnt.”

Sonja laughed and took another deep sip.

“So, why would a team of ghost hunters be interested in your barn anyway?” she asked, curious.

“Ghost hunters, huh?” he mumbled leaning on the table and sipping his coffee. “I suppose they think it's haunted.”

“Where did that rumor get started?”

“Oh, Marjorie started telling people about our ‘haunted barn’ while we were traveling the country a few years back.”

She remembered the year the Hinkley’s went off to roam the United States in an RV. She couldn’t have more than ten or eleven years old then.

“We were in Nevada or New Mexico. I can’t remember exactly which one. Both are big open deserts, both have casinos. We were sitting down to eat with some nice couple we had met at a blackjack table, and Marjorie went on this big, long tangent about how our barn was haunted. Claimed she'd seen a ghost once—hanging by its neck from the rafters."

Sonja suppressed a chill, and unconsciously reached back to pat down the hairs on the back of her neck. Just imagining a hanging body out in the barn gave her shivers. "Why would she say something like that?"

"Who knows? Craziest thing I'd ever heard her say. Before we bought the farm, there was a family who lived here that had a son, probably in his late teens. Apparently the young rascal decided he was in love with one of the girls in town. I think he wasn't quite "all there," if you know what I mean."

Sonja nodded.

"Well, anyway. From what we've heard, one night he tracked her down and tried to talk her into marrying him. When she told him 'no' he sort of lost it—grabbed her, tried to force her to say yes. Well, the fella didn't realize his own strength and killed her."

She shook her head, eyes wide. "That's awful."

"I personally think he meant to kill her, but Marjorie believed it was more sympathetic to the boy if she told the story that way," Mr. Hinkley shrugged. "Either way, the kid couldn't stand the guilt, and he knew the town would be after him, so he ran all the way here, back to the farm. He decided he didn't want to live with his guilt, and that he didn't want the townsfolk coming after him, so he strung himself up in the barn."

"He killed himself?" Sonja shuddered, feeling a sharp pang of sympathy for the young man, even if he had done something horrible.

"Yep, that's how the story goes."

"And Mrs. Hinkley thought she saw his ghost in the barn?"

"She did. And after the first time she mentioned it, she told that story to at least one person in every town we visited on that trip," he laughed. "She always did like to get a rise out of people."

"Yes, I suppose she did."

Sonja remembered one time on Halloween that Mrs. Hinkley had hung a fake body, just an old scarecrow or something, in the barn to scare all the kids. She'd never known that it was related to an actual story. The sound of a car driving up the dirt road drew their attention. Sonja sighed, hoping that it wasn't the Spirit Crew again.

"Who could that be?" Mr. Hinkley said. "I don't usually see a doggone soul out here."

The car stopped and a door opened and closed. Sonja stood up and headed over to where the front door stood open and felt her pulse pound, upon seeing the now-familiar white van out front. Couldn't they just leave well enough alone?

The young woman from the Spirit Crew approached and knocked on the frame of the door.

"Who is it?" Mr. Hinkley barked.

"I'll get this, don't worry," Sonja said in a low voice, approaching the screen door. "You were told that you couldn't film here," she called, not opening the screen.

"Sonja?" the woman asked.

"What do you need?"

"My name is Maddy—or Mystic, you can call me either one."

"What do you need, Maddy?" she asked sharply.

"I just wanted to come and apologize for the way we've treated you and Mr. Hinkley today," was the soft reply.

Sonja felt a hint of surprise at the comment. "Okay..." she said, still suspicious.

"Is it alright if I come in? I'd like to explain, you know, face to face?"

Sonja glanced back at Mr. Hinkley, who sighed, but nodded. "Let her in."

She opened the screen door.

"Alright, come in. You can have a cup of coffee with us."

———

"Thank you," Maddy said as Mr. Hinkley set the cup of coffee in front of her. She picked it up and took a sip before continuing. "Mmm...good."

Sonja wished she'd get to the point. While she appreciated Maddy coming to apologize, she'd had more than enough of the Spirit Crew for one day.

Maddy set down her mug.

"I am really sorry about what happened today, both here and at the diner. We didn't mean to cause any trouble."

Somehow, Sonja doubted that, at least from Spirit, but she let the 'mystic' continue.

"You see; we all care about the show so much."

"All of this for a television show?" Sonja raised a disapproving eyebrow.

"You don't understand. This show is our lives. We've poured everything we have into it, and—so far—it has paid off," the seemingly embarrassed girl took another sip of her coffee, trying to hide the flush that had risen on her cheeks.

"That's not exactly a valid excuse for bulldozing people to get what you want," Sonja pointed out.

Maddy set her coffee down. "Believe me, I know, but, Shelly . . . I mean Spirit, has really let it all go to his head.

"Shelly? Is that his real name?" the corner of Sonja's mouth twitched in amusement.

"Sheldon. We all have names we use on the show. Sheldon is Spirit. Tanner who manages the ghost detection equipment—is Tech, and I'm Mystic."

"Mystic?"

"Yes, because I can sense otherworldly forces—you know, I see ghosts."

Sonja's interest was piqued. While she still had her doubts about the truth of any content on a "reality" TV show, she was fascinated by and mildly frightened of the paranormal. She wondered if this young woman might have any insight that might help her understand the strange—potentially supernatural—experiences she'd had since her return to Haunted Falls.

"Ghosts? Hogwash," the skeptical farmer grumbled.

Sonja felt a bit sensitive about his comment. She had experienced a string of strange and potentially supernatural events of her own—all connected to the murder of local tycoon Ronda Smith, whose body had been dumped in the freezer at the diner. While the experiences had felt so real at the time, she doubted her own senses—and sanity—now that it was all over.

Maddy, on the other hand, seemed to honestly believe in the supernatural, and if she truly had a spiritual connection of some sort, Sonja wanted to know about it. At least, she hoped that the 'mystic' could help her feel less insane about the whole situation.

Maddy ignored Mr. Hinkley's disparaging comment and continued.

"I mean, only a few years ago Spirit was a struggling film student, working as a grocery store bagger. Back then, we only had our dreams. We filmed our ghost hunts for the heck of it - for fun mostly. Tech and I just thought of it as a hobby."

"How did you go from that to being the highest rated reality show on television?" Sonja was curious.

"We posted a few of our ghost hunts online. One of our videos went viral. In a matter of a few days over a million people had watched it. Then, next thing we knew, some big name producer was calling up Spirit and discussing turning our little videos into full-fledged television episodes."

Sonja nodded. "And the rest is history."

"The rest is history," Maddy affirmed, "but Spirit has gone kind of crazy lately. He's power and money hungry. All he wants is his next shot, but he doesn't want to jump through the hoops to get there."

"I see."

"I'm really very sorry about all this. Spirit had no right to act the way he did toward you."

Or anyone, Sonja thought.

Maddy looked as if she might cry.

"He works hard, but his personality and his temper just seem to rub everyone we meet the wrong way."

"And your team?"

Maddy nodded. "I honestly don't know how much more I can take."

A lightbulb went on in Sonja's head, connecting two and two. She sighed. "Are you romantically involved with Spirit?"

Maddy looked ashamed and nodded again. "Since before the show was picked up."

This girl seemed so sweet compared to Spirit. Sonja didn't understand why Maddy would date a man like that, and if he treated her the way he treated everyone else—well, there was really no reason for her to stay involved with him, but she immediately decided that that was none of her business.

"Look," she sighed, coming to a decision, "if Spirit is willing to go through the proper channels and get a permit, I'll allow him to film at the diner."

Maddy's eyes instantly lit up. "You will?"

Sonja nodded, while Mr. Hinkley looked at her like she was crazy.

"Oh, thank you, Sonja," she breathed.

"You're welcome."

The eager young woman looked at Hinkley, probably hoping he would give a similar offer, but the farmer remained stone silent and stared at her. Maddy understood.

"Thank you, again," she said, rising to go. "I'd better head out. Spirit doesn't know that I'm gone or that I borrowed the van."

"I'll walk you out," Sonja offered.

Mr. Hinkley remained at the table while the two women walked out the front door to the van.

"Do you think you could talk to him?" Maddy asked once they were far enough away from the farmhouse. "He seems to like you."

"Who? Mr. Hinkley?"

"Yeah, if we could shoot at the diner and here at the barn that would make things just perfect."

Sonja shook her head and folded her arms. "You have to understand, Maddy. Mr. Hinkley is an old man. He really just wants to be left alone. I doubt he'd budge on letting anyone film on his property."

"But it wouldn't hurt to at least talk to him, right?" she pleaded.

Sonja paused for a moment, giving the 'mystic' a long stare.

"Alright, I'll talk to him, but don't get your hopes up. I can tell you right now that he probably won't agree to it."

"Well, thank you for trying, anyway," Maddy smiled, opening the van door. "Oh, I had one more question. Do you think you could cater the shoot at the diner—and here if things work out?"

"I've never catered an event before," Sonja admitted. "The Waffle just opened today, but I'll certainly give it a try. Why not?"

"Thanks," Maddy sighed, giving the diner owner a hug before getting in the van.

"Can I ask you a question?" Sonja said.

"Sure, shoot."

"Can you really see and sense ghosts?"

Maddy smiled down at her.

"I sure can." She closed the door, started her engine, and pulled out of the drive.

Sonja looked up at the gray sky. It looked like a storm was coming.

CHAPTER FIVE

"Well, I'd better head back to the diner," Sonja told Mr. Hinkley, gathering her purse.

It was already around noon, and she needed to get back to The Waffle and help out. She could just imagine Vic and Alison drowning in customers and food orders.

"Something isn't right with that girl," Mr. Hinkley observed tartly. "No one in their right mind should be involved romantically with that rapscallion."

"It sounds like he wasn't always that way," Sonja tried to be optimistic.

"Folks tend to show their true colors the longer you know 'em."

Part of her wanted to agree with the old man.

"Either way, they're not going to film here. No way, no how. Not after the way that fella treated me—and you."

"He definitely seems to have difficulties interacting with people."

"He's downright crazy, if you ask me. I'm surprised you told that girl you would allow them to film at your diner."

"Well," she shrugged, "sometimes we just need to show a little charity, even if we don't want to."

The farmer looked at her skeptically but said nothing.

"Maddy deserves a chance even if Spirit doesn't."

"I guess we'll see about that," he muttered.

"Why not let them film here?" she asked. "After all, they'd only be filming in the barn."

"Nope, I already said no," the answer was instant.

"I'd be here to cater the shoot. I'd make sure that none of them came near the farmhouse."

"Not a chance," Mr. Hinkley insisted, stabbing his cane onto the wood floor.

"Would it really be that hard to just let them film for a couple of hours?" Sonja asked.

"Yes, it would, and I don't appreciate you asking on behalf of that young upstart," he frowned, his eyes filled with accusation. "Now, if you'll excuse me, I have some chores to do around the house." The old man grabbed the coffee cups from the table and put them none-too-gently in the sink. "You can show yourself out."

"I'm sorry, Mr. Hinkley," Sonja felt badly about having upset him.

"Go on now," he waved her off, his mouth pursed in a hard line.

"Sorry," she said again, kicking herself for ruining what had been a perfectly nice visit.

Sonja was back at the diner after the lunch rush had come and gone. She slipped in the back door and let out a long sigh.

"There you are," Alison exclaimed. "If only you'd been here thirty minutes ago."

"I'm so sorry," she replied, taking her apron off the hook and putting it on. "Things got a little hectic out at Hinkley's."

"What happened? Did Mr. Hinkley fill one of the Spirit Crew full of rock salt?" her friend teased.

Sonja reached up and pulled the next order off the turnstile so that Vic could take a break. "That's not funny, Ally."

"Sure, it is. I think it would be hilarious watching one of those smug jerks limp around with a butt full of rock salt."

"Well, Mr. Hinkley was really mad, but I kind of stepped in to handle things so that drastic measures like rock salt weren't necessary." She opened one of the refrigerators, pulled out a burger patty and threw it on the grill.

"What happened?"

"He told them to leave and they left, basically. It really wasn't a big deal."

"That's it?" she shook her head.

"He asked me to come in for some coffee afterwards."

Ally put her hands on her hips. "And you decided to do that instead of coming back to help with the lunch rush on opening day?" she challenged.

"Well, the girl from the crew came back."

"Maddy the Mystic?"

"Yep, she asked if I would talk to Mr. Hinkley and convince him to let them film there."

"And did you?"

"I tried," Sonja nodded. She still felt ashamed about having upset him.

"What did he say?"

"Well, Maddy apologized to him, and he seemed fairly content with the apology. He didn't say 'I accept' or 'you're forgiven' or anything, but he seemed content."

"That's about as good as can be expected from the cantankerous old guy," Ally pointed out.

"It wasn't until I came in and asked him to reconsider that he sort of went off the handle." Sonja flipped the sizzling burger. "He kicked me out."

Alison sighed. "Well, what did you expect?"

"I know, I just hate having contributed to him being upset. Hey, are there any fries on, Vic?" she called across the kitchen.

Vic nodded and dumped a tray of freshly chopped fries into the fryer. "Just started another batch."

"Anyways, she also asked if I could cater for them," Sonja remarked.

"She did?"

"And I told her I could do it."

"You did?"

She nodded. "And," Sonja smiled and looked her friend in the eye, "I said they could film here,"

"Ha, I knew it," Alison clapped her hands. "That's so exciting. Your diner will be on television all over the world."

"Our diner will be on television all over the world," Sonja reminded her.

"And we'll probably be on television too. They always interview the owners," Ally's eyes sparkled.

Sonja nodded. She had to admit, she was surprised to find herself becoming more excited about the whole thing.

"You can't get better advertising than that," Ally exclaimed.

Sonja had to agree.

It was around eight thirty when Sonja was finally getting ready to close up. The last customer left around eight and she locked the door behind them. She decided to make a few Cinnamon Attack Waffles before she left, figuring that she'd take the waffles as a peace offering to Mr. Hinkley. They were probably one of the unhealthiest—and yet most dangerously delicious—items served at the diner.

She poured the batter into the waffle iron, letting it cook until it had a perfect nutmeg-brown exterior, and when it was done, she took it out of the iron and brushed it with melted butter, dipping the decadent waffle in a bowl of cinnamon sugar, turning it over and over until it was coated on all sides.

When she topped that luscious creation with ice cream and a decorative chocolate drizzle, she'd have customers drooling with anticipation.

Grabbing a tub of ice cream and the chocolate sauce on her way out the door, Sonja headed for the car. She couldn't bring herself to just let the ice cream melt and ruin the waffles before she got there. She drove away from the diner, and had a jarring moment when she realized it might be too late in the evening for Mr. Hinkley, and he might already be in bed. If the lights were on when she arrived, she would knock, if not, she would just take the waffles home to her mother—she'd love them.

As Sonja drove toward the farm, it had just barely started to rain, sprinkling her windshield with silvery droplets. By the time she reached the canal bridge, the storm was in full force. Rain came down in torrents, blurring her windshield. Even with the wipers turned up to full speed, it was difficult to see. The canal was swelling, almost touching the underside of the bridge, and for a moment, Sonja considered turning back and just heading home, but she was almost to her destination anyway, so she pushed on toward the farmhouse.

As the car crested the drive and the farmhouse and barn came into view she felt her heart drop. There, parked behind the barn, was the white van. It was just out of sight so that it wouldn't be seen from the farmhouse, but she could see it clearly from the road. Sonja couldn't believe it. She had given Maddy the benefit of the doubt and her kindness had been met with dishonesty.

Sonja parked her car right next to the van, blocking it in, and pulled out her cell phone. She dialed the police station and informed Sheriff Thompson of the situation. He told her to stay put and to not do anything until he got there, but Sonja couldn't just sit by, not after they had betrayed her trust. She got out of her car, the rain quickly soaking her to the skin, and headed for the barn.

CHAPTER SIX

Sonja wished she still had the emergency poncho or an umbrella in the car as she walked through the downpour to the rear entrance of the barn. She stopped just outside the door and listened. It was difficult to hear over the thunder and torrents of rain, but she could partially make out Spirit's voice as he narrated what was happening around them. Not waiting another moment, she opened the doors and stepped in. There was a gasp. The bright light of the camera turned and shone in her eyes.

"Get that light out of my face," she ordered.

"It looks like we have an unexpected guest," Spirit narrated stepping closer. "The local diner owner, most likely sensitive to supernatural happenings herself, has just arrived."

"What do you think you're doing?" Sonja demanded. "And, I said, get that light out of my face," she glared.

Instantly, the light turned off.

"Hey, what are you doing?" Spirit shouted at his team. "Keep filming."

The light came back on and the host went on narrating as if nothing had happened. "It was here in this very barn that the young man hung himself."

Sonja stepped in and pushed the camera away, taking the cameraman by surprise. "Turn that off. You have no right to film in here."

"Stop interrupting the shoot," Spirit ordered, through his teeth. "How am I ever going to finish this episode if you keep interrupting?"

"You don't have permission to shoot here," she yelled back, raising her voice over the gale outside. "You need to pack up your van and leave. Now."

"No way," he shook his head. "We aren't leaving until we get this section of the episode done."

“Come on,” Maddy called out. “She’s right. We shouldn’t have even come here.”

“Do you want to get this footage or not?” the belligerent young man asked incredulously.

Maddy hung her head.

“Come on, let’s shoot this,” Spirit ignored his girlfriend and spoke to the cameraman.

Sonja couldn’t believe the gall of this jerk. She was at her wits end, and if Sheriff Thompson didn’t show up soon she might just lose it. Suddenly, the front door of the barn burst open. Mr. Hinkley stood in the rain, a shotgun in his hand.

“Everybody out of my barn now.”

“You’ve got to be kidding me,” Spirit ran a hand through his hair, enraged. “Will you people just get out of my way and let me shoot my episode?”

The furious farmer hobbled into the room. When he spotted Sonja, his eyes grew wide.

“Sonja?”

"Mr. Hinkley, I was trying to get them out of here."

His expression went from hurt, back to angry.

"I don't care who was doing what. You're all trespassing. If you don't get your keisters out of here right now, I'm gonna start shooting."

"Come on, Tech," Spirit ordered. "Let's get this filming done.

"He has a shotgun, Spirit," he protested. None of them knew that it probably only had rock salt in it. It would hurt, but wouldn't do any serious damage.

"This geezer isn't shooting anyone. Bring the Seer device over here."

"I'm not so sure about that, Spirit," Tech kept casting wary glances toward Mr. Hinkley.

"Do it, NOW," the brash star shouted.

"You do it," Tech yelled.

He leaned over and grabbed a pouch from a stack of production equipment.

"I'm not getting shot for you, man."

He pulled a strange flat-screen item—which Sonja assumed was the Seer—out of the pouch and held it up, prepared to toss it at Spirit.

A thudding sound in the rafters interrupted the argument. A large figure leaped down from the loft and knocked Tech to the ground, knocking the wind out of him.

The camera's light revealed the assailant's identity. It was Daniel Marston. The elder ghost hunter moved to kick the Seer out of the pouch that was by Tech's leg, misfired and kicked the unsuspecting crew member instead. There was an audible snap and Tech screamed out in pain.

Sonja ran to the beast of a man and pummeled his arm with her fists.

"Stop it," she cried out.

"I think he broke my leg," Tech shouted clutching the throbbing limb.

Daniel pushed Sonja aside without even realizing he had done it, focusing on retrieving the Seer. She fell heavily onto a bale of hay.

A loud blast boomed through the barn, seeming to shake the sides. Everyone froze, immediately going silent. Mr. Hinkley held the shotgun pointed up in the air. Sonja was thankful that the sound had stopped Daniel's vicious assault.

They heard a siren and saw the flash of lights as Sheriff Thompson pulled up just outside the barn.

"Put your shotgun down, Sam," Sheriff Thompson ordered, appearing in the doorway.

The old farmer obeyed, lowering the shotgun. "It's only got rock salt in it," he muttered.

"I don't care what it's got in it," was the stern reply. The sheriff saw Sonja sprawled on a hay bale and his jaw flexed. "You okay?"

"I think so," she nodded, slowly making her way to her feet.

"I already warned the rest of you once today that I didn't want any more trouble. Looks like you couldn't follow basic instructions even for a few hours. I'm taking you all in and booking you for trespassing in the morning."

The sheriff glanced at Tech, writhing on the ground. "What happened here?" he asked, his eyes narrowing.

Spirit walked over and tried to pull Tech up, but the crew member curled up and cried out in pain.

"Sheriff," Maddy said. "That guy kicked Tech and broke his leg," she pointed at Daniel.

The officer looked at Daniel. "Is that true?"

The defiant middle aged man merely glowered silently at Thompson, not saying a word.

The sheriff turned to the rest of the group. "Is it true?"

Everyone nodded.

Then he looked at Sonja. "Sonja?"

"It's true," she confirmed. "He jumped on top of him from the loft and then kicked his leg."

"They have something that belongs to me," Daniel shouted defensively. "I was just trying to get back what is rightfully mine. You're an officer of the law. You need to make him give me back my property."

"You're about to be charged with assault and battery," Sheriff Thompson replied calmly. "If I hear one more word out of you I will not hesitate to lock you in the squad car for the rest of the night, while I sort the rest of this mess out," he declared, meaning it.

Daniel's head drooped low, and Thompson took him by the arm.

"Alright," he ordered, "everybody into the farmhouse."

"The farmhouse?" Mr. Hinkley protested. "They can't come in my farmhouse."

"They're going to have to," the sheriff replied. "That leg is going to need treatment, and we're going to get this young man out of the weather while we're waiting for help to arrive."

"Then take him back across the river to the hospital," the

farmer blustered. “I won’t have these trespassers in my house. Absolutely not.”

Sheriff Thompson loomed over the farmer and looked him in the eye. “I’m afraid we don’t have any other choice, Sam. The bridge washed out behind me when I came across. No one is getting out tonight.”

CHAPTER SEVEN

Sheriff Thompson led Daniel into the front door of the farmhouse, while crew members mostly carried Tech in behind him.

"Do you have a room that locks from the outside?" he asked Mr. Hinkley.

"Sure, the cellar locks from the outside."

"I guess that'll have to do," the sheriff shrugged.

Daniel's eyes widened. "You can't lock me in the cellar all night long."

"Sure I can, and it's our only option at this point." He turned to Mr. Hinkley. "I want you to grab some blankets and pillows for him. Do you have a cot?"

"Yeah, in the attic."

"Go ahead and get it. Where's the cellar key?"

"In the kitchen drawer next to the cellar door."

"Alright."

Thompson led the assailant away while Maddy and Spirit helped Tech into the living room and onto the couch.

"No, take him to the upstairs guest bedroom," the farmer ordered as he walked through the room and up the stairs. "I don't want him on the couch."

"I need my bag," Tech pleaded. "It's got some painkillers in it."

"Okay, I'll get it," Maddy promised, running back out into the storm.

Sonja sighed and looked at Spirit. "Alright, I'll help you get him upstairs." She positioned herself under Tech's arm and they took him upstairs. A few moments later Maddy came into the guest bedroom holding the duffle bag.

"Thanks, Maddy," Tech groaned, his face white with pain. He shuffled through the bag, pulling out different bottles, clothes, a book, and finally the painkillers. "I-I think I need to use the bathroom really quick."

Sonja sighed, "Alright, get him up again."

"You couldn't have thought of that before we plopped you down on the bed?" Spirit complained.

"Just help," she ordered.

They hauled him to the bathroom and a few minutes later back to the bedroom again.

"Now, let's look at your leg," Sonja instructed. "Can you pull up your pant leg?"

Slowly, painfully, Tech pulled the pants up. Underneath was a gigantic red and purple bruise. "It doesn't look as bad as it could be," she said. "Let's get your boots off."

"Don't touch it," Tech cried.

"I won't. Don't worry," Sonja said.

Maddy began unlacing the boots. Carefully, she pulled them off and set them on the floor.

"Maddy, go get some ice from the freezer downstairs, and bring it back up here," Sonja directed.

The young woman nodded and headed out.

"Okay, hand me those pillows," she told Spirit, pointing at the pile of pillows on the chair in the corner. "We need to elevate this."

She propped up the leg carefully on the pillows. "How are you feeling?" He didn't respond. He was already asleep.

———

After elevating both of Tech's feet, just in case he may have symptoms of shock, Sonja stepped out of the room and let out her breath in a whoosh. She needed to be alone.

She made her way down the narrow hall and entered the last bedroom on the right. Standing in the darkness of the room, she just let herself breathe quietly. The entire day had turned out far more eventful than she had expected—and not in a good way. The Waffle's grand opening had been an exciting event, now completely overshadowed by the Spirit Crew and their Hollywood drama.

Sonja wanted to cry. Half her day had been spent running around Haunted Falls instead of working at The Waffle with Alison and Vic, where she belonged. As the owner, she knew she was the official face of The Waffle, and yet she hadn't even been there for much of the day. She'd also managed to offend an old friend of the family—Mr. Hinkley—by getting involved with the Spirit Crew. She only hoped she could gain his trust and confidence back.

Maddy had really let her down, too. The most logical explanation seemed to be that Maddy was just too weak to stand up to Spirit when he demanded something. Unfortunately, his most recent demand involved illegally trespassing and filming on Mr. Hinkley's land. Now, they'd all have to pay the consequences. Tech was already paying with a broken leg. That other character, Daniel, had thrown himself in the mix and would most likely be charged with assault.

It had been a stressful day for all the wrong reasons, and now she couldn't even go home and stand under the steamy warmth of a hot shower and lay in bed afterward watching old noir films until she fell asleep. Instead, the exhausted and worn-down diner owner was stuck here in this farmhouse with a group of very tense people.

She sat on the edge of the bed in the room and stared out the window into the dark and rainy night. She felt herself drifting, caught in the final moments of exhaustion from a long and stressful day. For just a moment, she closed her eyes.

Sonja was lying down. It was still dark and raining. She knew she had fallen asleep but didn't know when. She sat up, wondering what time it was, and looked around the room for a clock. There was none that she could see.

She blinked sleepily, rubbed her eyes, and stood up to look out the window, when something caught her eye. She peered out, watching as someone moved around in the loft of the barn. Who on earth would be out there in this wretched weather? Maybe it was Spirit desperately trying to defiantly steal a few shots.

Sonja squinted trying to make out who it was standing there, and the figure turned to face her. She felt her heart leap in her chest and the blood run cold in her veins. Even through the rain-streaked glass, she could make out the figure's sickeningly pale complexion. Its face gave off a bluish glow and was translucent. Its eyes pierced her to the core, sending chills up and down her spine.

Sonja hurried down the stairs to the main floor of the house and ran out the door into the pouring rain. She heard Sheriff Thompson call to her from within the farmhouse, but didn't stop. Keeping her eye on the loft, she searched desperately for the apparition that she had seen from the window, but it was gone. She ran and pushed open the front door of the barn and stepped in. It was dark inside and difficult to see.

As she moved through the damp, dark interior, she felt something brush against her face, and leaped back with a gasp. Her blood ran cold, and she whimpered in fear. Lightning flashed, illuminating the barn and revealing what she had just touched. Spirit's limp, lifeless body hung from the rafters of the barn, a piece of electrical cord tied around his neck.

CHAPTER EIGHT

Sheriff Thompson ran in behind Sonja. "What are you doing out here?" he asked, as she burrowed into his side, fear overcoming her.

The lightning flashed again and the sheriff stopped dead in his tracks.

"Is that Spirit?" he asked grimly.

She nodded, without looking back at the body. "It is."

"Quick, help me get him down from there."

She blinked at him for a moment, then snapped out of it. "Do you have a light?"

"Here." He pulled a small flashlight from his belt and turned it on. She took it from him and found the ladder leading up to the loft. She quickly climbed to the top, moving over and locating the beam where the wire was tied. It was wrapped around the beam and knotted tightly. She struggled with it for a moment.

"I can't get this undone," she grimaced, trying not to think of what dangled at the other end of the wire.

"Here," Thompson called out, expertly tossing a pocket knife up to her.

She caught it and cut through the wire. Sheriff Thompson held Spirit in his arms and gently let him down onto the dirt floor.

Sonja rushed down the ladder to see what was happening.

He took the light back from Sonja to look Spirit over. He was clearly dead. The body was pale and the eyes were wide open and bulging from their sockets. The sheriff leaned in, listening for breath. He placed two fingers against Spirit's neck, checking for a pulse.

But Sonja knew it was too late.

"He's dead," Thompson confirmed quietly.

She sighed, overwhelmed. This was the second dead body she had found since her return to Haunted Falls. And then there was the figure that she had seen in the loft. All of the strange, potentially supernatural, experiences from the previous week came flooding back to her. She had started to convince herself that none of it had ever actually happened, assured herself that she was simply being hysterical, but this time—this time—the frightened diner owner was almost positive she had seen a ghost.

Had she seen Spirit's ghost, calling to her, trying to let her know that he was dead?

She looked at the sad, still form lying in the dirt and noticed something in his hand. "What's that?" she pointed.

Using a handkerchief from his pocket Sheriff Thompson carefully reached down and pulled a piece of paper from the hand and unfolded it.

"What is it?" she asked.

He held it out so she could read the writing. Sonja's eyes widened.

"We better find Maddy."

Sonja went back into the house and hurried upstairs to find Maddy. In the guest bedroom, Tech was still asleep. He looked pale, was drenched in sweat, and his leg looked far more swollen than before. It was obviously getting worse and needed more ice. Sonja also noticed that Tech's feet were bare now. Maddy sat by the bed stroking his soaked hair.

"His socks were muddy and soaked through," the young woman said, noticing Sonja staring. "So, I hung them over that chair." She pointed at the cane chair in the corner. A pair of brown, muddy socks hung there.

"Sonja?" Maddy said, looking up with a concerned expression. "Are you alright? You look upset. Is something wrong?"

"Sheriff Thompson needs you downstairs," Sonja finally replied.

"Why?"

"He'll explain once you get down there."

"Alright," young woman agreed, worried.

Sonja followed her downstairs into the living room. The note lay open on the coffee table in front of the couch. Sheriff Thompson sat in an easy chair near the fireplace on the other side of the coffee table.

"Have a seat, Maddy."

Sonja stood off to the side, waiting to see what would happen next.

"Is this your handwriting?" He asked, gesturing to the note.

Maddy leaned over, peering at it. "Maybe?" She read the handwriting. "But . . . I-I don't remember writing this."

"But it is your handwriting?"

"Well, it looks similar," Maddy confirmed, "but it can't be mine. I didn't write this."

"You didn't ask Spirit to meet you outside in the barn tonight?"

"No." Her answer sounded more like a question itself. "What is this all about?"

"Where were you during the last hour?"

She paused for a moment, bewildered, then answered.

"I came in and helped Sonja get Tech's leg set up, then I got some ice for him. After that I went to the bathroom and took a pretty long shower, I just kind of stood in there for a while, you know, trying to let the water wash away the day. Then, I went back and sat next to Tech."

"That's where I found her," Sonja verified.

Sheriff Thompson gave Sonja a look before continuing on.

"You were in the shower? Did anyone else know you were in the shower?"

"No. I just felt like I needed one."

"Did Mr. Hinkley know?"

"No. If he's mad, I'm sorry. I knew that he was kind of upset, so I didn't want to bother him by asking."

The officer nodded.

"Sheriff, shouldn't you tell her?" Sonja asked, trying to be helpful.

Sheriff Thompson raised his eyebrows to silence her.

"Tell me what?" Maddy asked.

Sheriff Thompson looked her directly in the eye. "Spirit is dead."

All the color drained from Maddy's face. "What?"

"He was found in the barn."

Tears welled and trickled down her cheeks in forlorn streams. "He...he's...dead?"

"I'm afraid so."

"But...how...what happened?" she asked.

"We aren't sure yet," the sheriff replied.

"It could have been murder," Sonja chimed in, eyes wide.

The sheriff sighed. "Sonja? Will you please wait in the other room?"

Sonja didn't budge.

"Someone killed him?" Maddy asked, horror in her eyes.

The officer grimaced. "It's a possibility," he said. "There'll need to be an investigation."

The frightened girl was shaking, "And you think I did it? B-because of this note?" She said, pointing at the note on the table.

"I haven't formed any theories yet," he assured her.

Her shaking was getting worse. Sonja stepped in, "I think she's going into shock." She moved quickly over to the grief-stricken young woman. "Maddy, you need to lie down."

Sonja grabbed a sofa cushion and put it under her feet. "We'll need a cold compress of some sort." She stood up and headed into the bathroom. Sheriff Thompson followed.

"It has to be murder," she whispered, opening cabinets in search of a clean washcloth or towel.

"Sonja, it's way too soon to be drawing those types of conclusions."

"He couldn't have jumped from the loft," she paused, "his neck wasn't broken."

"Well, I'll have to actually take a look around when it's light out," the sheriff commented. "I don't want everyone in the house going into a panic. For right now, he died in an accident. Got it?"

Sonja nodded. "Got it." She couldn't find washcloths anywhere in the bathroom. It shouldn't have been a surprise, since Mr. Hinkley rarely had guests.

"Sonja, I need to ask you something."

Sonja stopped cold. Oddly, she suddenly imagined him

getting close, asking if she maybe wanted to grab a bite to eat sometime. She could totally see Alison talking to him, putting him up to it. "What's that?"

"If this does turn out to be a murder, I don't want you to try to get involved."

Sonja sighed inwardly, not knowing whether she was relieved or disappointed.

"I'm a witness." she reminded him. "I found the body and that note. I think I'm already involved."

"I just don't want you trying to help," he said, placing a warm hand on her shoulder. I also don't want you getting hurt, Sonja imagined him saying. After all, there had been attempts on her life before.

She shook her head, trying to clear it. She was letting what Alison had said earlier get to her.

"What about Maddy?"

"She is my only suspect at the moment."

"What about everyone else in the house?" Sonja argued. "We

all had an equal opportunity."

"I'll have to get statements from everyone. But first I need to make sure whether this is actually a murder before I do anything else."

She nodded. "I don't think there are any washcloths in here."

"Let's try the kitchen," Sheriff Thompson suggested.

They walked out of the bathroom and into the kitchen.

"What's going on?" Mr. Hinkley asked. He was sitting at the table, his shotgun in front of him.

"Will you put that thing away?" Sheriff Thompson shook his head.

"I'm making sure that guy in the basement doesn't get away."

"He's not going anywhere," the sheriff held out his hand. "Give me the shotgun."

"I have a right to protect my home," the old coot argued.

"I know you've used this once tonight, Sam. Give me the shotgun now and I won't take it away for good."

The old man grunted as he pushed the shotgun across the table.

"I'm taking this and keeping it until we are all gone. Then you can have it back."

"Ain't hurting nothing," Mr. Hinkley complained.

Sheriff Thompson ignored him and headed over to Sonja. She reached for the dish towel from behind the sink and ran it under cold water. "I guess we'll just use this for now."

"What now?" Mr. Hinkley asked.

"There's been an accident," Thompson replied.

The farmer looked a bit alarmed. "One of those durn fool kids?"

The officer nodded. "Yes, one of the film crew."

Suddenly, Benjamin came in from the study. "Did you say there was an accident?"

"I'm sorry, who are you again?" Thompson asked.

"I'm Benjamin Simon, the cameraman for the Spirit Crew."

"Well, Benjamin," Thompson said, "there's been an accident."

"Is it bad? What happened?" he asked urgently.

"Yes, it's bad," Sonja nodded somberly. "Spirit is dead."

The cameraman's jaw dropped "Spirit is dead?"

"Alright," Sheriff Thompson quickly intervened. "Look, we don't know what exactly happened yet, but I'll need to get statements from all of you in the morning."

"You mean we have to stick around town?" Benjamin asked.

"That's correct, no one who was here on the farm tonight can leave town until this whole thing is cleared up," the sheriff verified, "but for right now, I want everyone to get a little shut-eye. Tomorrow is going to be a long day."

“How do you expect me to sleep after telling me that one of us is dead and you don’t know what’s going on?” Benjamin was aghast.

“I know, it’s rough, and I’m sorry, but it’s the best we can do for now. I’ll know more in the morning,” Sheriff Thompson headed out into the living room.

“Do the others know?” Benjamin was wide-eyed and shaken.

“Maddy knows,” Sonja replied.

Somehow she knew she wouldn’t be sleeping at all that night.

CHAPTER NINE

In the early hours of the morning, the storm finally cleared up. Sonja had tried to sleep, but was ultimately unsuccessful. As the first rays of daylight brushed the sky, she got up from the lounge chair on which she had been tossing and turning all night. Needless to say, she was ready to get away from the Hinkley farm and back to normal life. The whole night seemed like an awkward nightmare.

She finally remembered the waffles and ice cream she had intended to give to Mr. Hinkley the night before—which was the entire reason for making the trip out. By now, the waffles would be soggy and stale and the ice cream melted. Luckily, it was in a plastic container and hopefully wouldn't have gotten all over her car.

Sonja walked into the kitchen to get a glass of water. Muffled sounds seemed to come from behind the study door. She drank down the glass in huge gulps, then knocked on the door. The muffled noises stopped and someone moved around, shuffling something back and forth, then the door opened. Benjamin stood there, looking just as tired as Sonja felt.

"Oh, hi," he smiled wanly. "Sonja, right?"

"That's right," she nodded, smiling back. "I heard noises in here."

"Oh, yeah, I was just reviewing some of the footage from last night," he motioned to the desk where he had some equipment set up.

"Oh?"

"Yeah, mostly trying to see what happened when Daniel Marston dropped in and assaulted Tech."

Sonja bit her bottom lip and then asked, "Do you mind if I have a look at it with you?"

She felt her heart flutter in her chest, but in a good way. It was a sensation she hadn't felt in quite a while.

Benjamin let out a breath, "I guess not, but I'm not sure what there is to see."

He stepped into the room and sat back down at the desk. Sonja walked in and shut the door behind herself. The cameraman had a small setup of equipment on the desk. A laptop sat open, connected to the camcorder. Wires ran between the two devices.

Sonja moved around the desk and looked at the laptop. A still image from inside the barn sat on the screen. The image was filtered in green. Night vision, Sonja guessed.

"So, this is from last night?" she asked again, pretending to be ignorant.

"Yep," Benjamin replied. "Let me just rewind a little." He pulled back on the progress tab at the bottom of the video. "This is just before Daniel dropped in from the rafters." He hit the play button. Sonja watched Spirit, still alive and well, yelling at the camera.

The image spun, catching Daniel just as he toppled out of the rafters. Tech went down, apparently trying to protect The Seer that was still in his hands.

Daniel kicked Tech's leg. In the video, Tech screamed and moaned. "Go back again," Sonja instructed.

Benjamin did, rewinding the video and then pressing play.

She leaned in to get a better look at the screen and felt her arm brush Benjamin's. Goosebumps tickled her skin. She tried to ignore the sensation and pay attention to the video.

Daniel dropped down and kicked Tech's leg again. Tech screamed.

"It's amazing that with just that one kick, Daniel was able to break Tech's leg," she commented.

"Yeah, I knew the guy was big, but with that kind of strength, I would not want to go head to head with him."

Tech's leg looked so mangled the night before. The swelling and bruising only seemed to intensify as the night had gone on. She figured that Daniel must be extremely strong. It frightened her to think of what kind of damage he could do if he really wanted to.

If he hadn't been locked up in the cellar all night long she would have instantly singled him out as the main suspect in the killing. He had the motive and the strength, that was for sure.

"It surprised me that Spirit decided to go toe to toe with

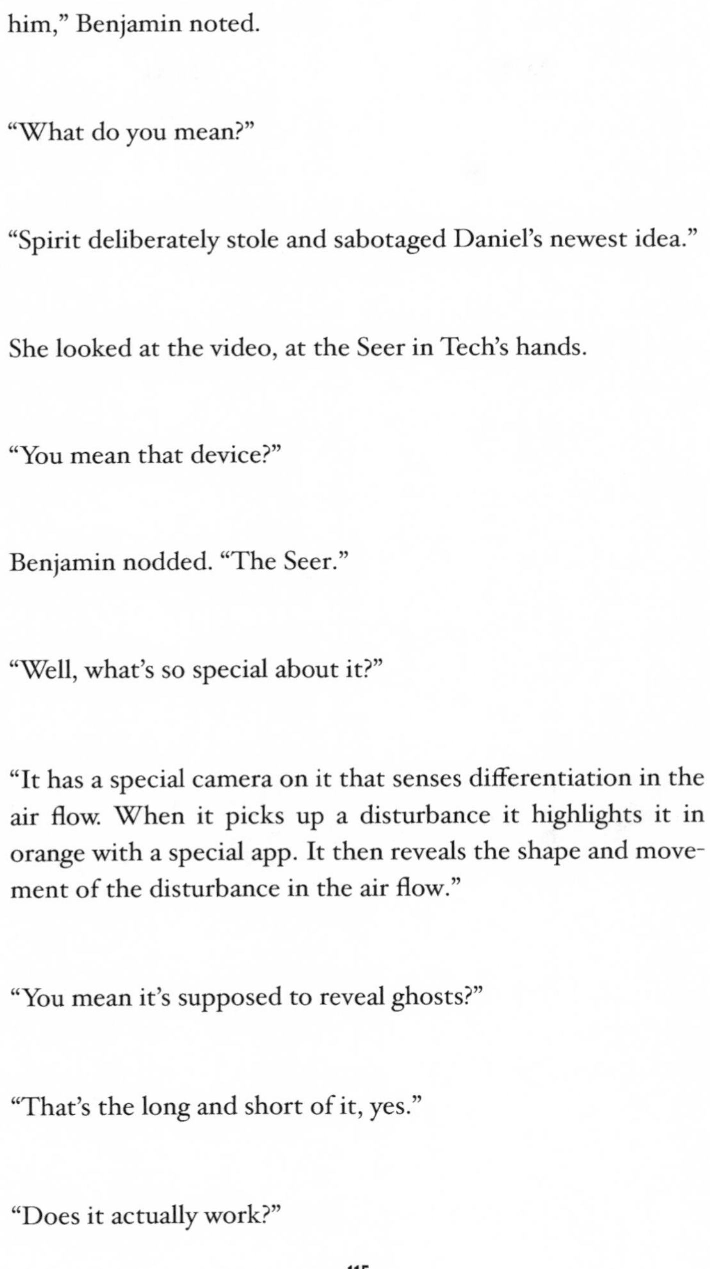

him," Benjamin noted.

"What do you mean?"

"Spirit deliberately stole and sabotaged Daniel's newest idea."

She looked at the video, at the Seer in Tech's hands.

"You mean that device?"

Benjamin nodded. "The Seer."

"Well, what's so special about it?"

"It has a special camera on it that senses differentiation in the air flow. When it picks up a disturbance it highlights it in orange with a special app. It then reveals the shape and movement of the disturbance in the air flow."

"You mean it's supposed to reveal ghosts?"

"That's the long and short of it, yes."

"Does it actually work?"

Benjamin smiled mischievously.

"Of course not. It's just a gimmick to increase ratings on the show. The device actually does pick up disturbances in the air flow of a room. But after that, the program basically makes out a shape that is intended to trick viewers into thinking it's a ghost. It's a smoke screen, just like everything else we do on the show."

"So, everything you guys do is fake?" Sonja asked.

"Of course it is," he replied with a nod. "None of it's real. Reality TV is all a sham. But," he shrugged, "the viewers eat it up."

"And all of your equipment that appears on camera is mostly for show."

"You got it. In fact, I often set up different tricks, sound effect boxes, strings on doors, stuff like that before a shoot even begins. I find that creating the environment—organically on camera—makes a far more convincing experience than using computer editing afterward."

"I see," Sonja remarked.

She was honestly disappointed. Lately, she had felt insane with how many ghostly things she had seen herself. In fact, she had seen—what looked like—a ghost at the diner twice now. She had honestly believed for a while that it was the ghost of Ronda Smith, the woman who had died there. She'd also experienced seeing quite the frightening "apparition" during a séance only a few nights ago. Add last night's apparition in the barn on top of that and this small town diner owner felt like a grade-A nutcase. Sonja had honestly hoped that by agreeing to let them film and investigate at the diner that they would find something that proved what she had seen was real. Then she wouldn't feel quite so paranoid.

"Does any of the team actually believe in the supernatural?"

"I don't," Benjamin commented, "and I'm pretty sure all the others are faking it. To be honest, it isn't just the ghosts they are faking. They fake their relationships, too. It's all one big sham to get higher ratings."

"I see," she bit her lip.

Perhaps Maddy was just an excellent actress, faking her way through every conversation they'd had together.

"After the dust from all of this settles, I think I'm about done with television," the cameraman confided.

"What do you mean?"

"Well, these three kids, they're the biggest pains in the petunias that I've ever had to work with. After dealing with them on this show I think I'm just about done with television and movies altogether."

"And what would you do instead?"

Benjamin pushed back from the desk and walked over to the window. "I'd probably choose to live someplace like this."

Sonja felt her heart leap in her chest. The thought of him living in Haunted Falls, close to her, was exciting. She might even consider the prospect of dating again.

"I'd like to work on a farm, do something meaningful with my life," he mused. He turned and looked at Sonja. "Now that Spirit is dead, they'll probably cancel the show. I might finally get my chance to escape."

CHAPTER TEN

Within a few hours of everyone waking up, a rescue team was able to get the bridge back up and functional. The paramedics came in to work on Tech, and it turned out that he had a high fever to go along with his broken leg, so they quickly loaded him up and rushed him off to the Haunted Falls Hospital.

Maddy wanted to go along with Tech, but Sheriff Thompson wouldn't allow it. She was a suspect and the sheriff was planning on taking her in for questioning as soon as he finished examining the crime scene. His deputies cordoned off the investigation area with the usual yellow tape and got right to work.

Sonja wanted to believe that the young woman was innocent, but after what Benjamin had said about the whole team being a sham, she worried that she had been deceived.

Daniel was retrieved from the cellar, but Tech said he wasn't going to press charges. That surprised everyone, especially Maddy, and it meant that Daniel could just walk away.

"Don't leave town," Sheriff Thompson instructed Daniel as they stood on the front drive of the farmhouse. "I still need to question you later on about Spirit's death."

"Why do I need to stay around?" he demanded. "I was locked in that spider-infested hole all night, and I have a class to teach back in LA tomorrow afternoon."

"A class?" Sonja inquired, standing on the farmhouse porch.

"I train and certify professional stuntmen on the side for extra cash."

That explained why he was so fit and strong.

"I don't care if you have a meeting with the President of the United States," Sheriff Thompson replied. "We'll still need your statement before you leave town."

Daniel's face darkened ominously. "If you're accusing me of killing that little twerp, you couldn't be more wrong. You locked me in the cellar, I couldn't have done it."

That was true, Sonja thought. How could he have done it?

"No one is accusing you of anything, but I'll need to get your statement before you leave."

"I'm a free citizen of the United States of America. You have no right to order me to stay in this little nothing town."

"Well," the officer retorted, "If you choose to leave before I can question you, I have no other choice than to believe you were somehow involved in Spirit's death."

Daniel scowled, but realized that he didn't have a choice.

"Fine, but once this is over I am out of here for good."

"Thank heaven for that," the sheriff groaned. He turned toward Sonja. "And what did I say about becoming involved?"

"Sorry," she apologized. "You haven't interviewed me yet."

Sheriff Thompson chuckled. "Don't worry. I'll get your statement along with everyone else's," he replied. "After all, you did find the body."

“That’s what I said last night.”

“I’m aware.”

“Well. I promise not to skip out of town,” Sonja teased.

“I’m not worried about it.”

One of the deputies came out of the barn, stepping under the yellow caution tape. “Well, Sheriff. I’d say there is no way that guy could have killed himself. There was not a single thing nearby he could have jumped off of.”

“What about jumping from the loft itself?”

“Not with the way the wire was tied up there. It looked like someone needed to actually pull on one end to lift the guy up. He couldn’t have done that himself.”

“Alright,” the sheriff said. “Let me know if you find anything else.”

Sonja folded her arms and stared at Sheriff Thompson. “So, it was murder.”

He sighed. "Looks that way. But, remember," he said shaking a finger, "just keep your nose out of it."

Sonja finally left the farm and immediately headed for The Waffle. She at least needed to check in on things before she ran home, took a shower, and changed her clothes.

As she drove, Maddy was still on her mind. Sonja's gut feeling was that Maddy was telling the truth, that she wasn't just acting. After all, Maddy had reached out and apologized after the incident at the diner. She hoped that the young woman had nothing to do with the murder. Perhaps the note found on the body was just a coincidence—or it was planted. Either way, she wouldn't know for sure if Maddy was telling the truth or not, not until she talked to her again.

Pulling into the diner, she was amazed at the number of cars in the parking lot. It seemed that The Waffle had drawn a whole round of returning customers the second day. She quickly parked the car, headed around the building and walked in the back door.

Vic looked up from the egg frying on the griddle, smiled and waved.

"Hi, Vic."

"Hi, Sonja," he beamed. "Alison," Vic called into the dining area. "Sonja's here."

"About time," Alison shouted from the front.

"I thought Alex was running grill today," she said.

"He told Alison he wanted another day at home with Cynthia, so here I am," the jolly cook shrugged.

Sonja thanked her lucky stars for such a great team of employees who worked hard and didn't hold a grudge over the fact that she had been gone for so long.

Within seconds, Alison appeared in the back. "Here you are. Where were you this morning when we opened?"

"I'm sorry, it's a long story" she apologized.

Her friend gave her the up and down look. "You look like you haven't slept a wink. Are you okay?"

"I haven't slept at all," Sonja admitted. "I was out at Hinkley's farm all night. The bridge washed out."

"Washed out?" Ally remarked, surprised. "And you got stuck out there?"

"Yeah, me and the Spirit Crew."

"You're kidding."

"I caught them trying to film without permission."

"Well, I bet that was just a blast."

"Actually," Sonja confided, "one of them is dead."

After recounting the night's many details and events Sonja asked Alison and Vic if they could cover for her while she got some shut eye. They agreed, of course, and called in a relief server to help out while Alison worked in the kitchen. Once everything was settled, Sonja headed home and hopped in the shower, washed off, then fell right into bed, sleeping for around four hours. It was already three in the afternoon by the time she woke up.

Sonja got out of bed, got dressed, and headed over to the police station hoping Maddy would still be there. She knew Sheriff Thompson had instructed her to not put her nose where it didn't belong, but she just felt like she needed to talk to Maddy one more time. She walked into the police station and asked if the young woman was there.

Marie, the older gal at the front desk, said, “Sure, hon. She’s still here. The sheriff has her in the holding cell.”

“The holding cell,” Sonja exclaimed. “Why is she in there?”

“Probable cause, apparently.”

“Darn,” she sighed. Now she felt guilty, like she should have come right over after leaving the farm instead of sleeping. “Is it possible for me to see her?”

“Well, hon, you’d have to get Sheriff Thompson’s permission for that.”

“Well, where is he?”

“He’s interviewing that cameraman fellow right now. I’m not sure when he’ll be out.”

“Marie, I need to talk to Maddy.”

“Well, dear. I’m not sure how I can help.”

Sonja paused a moment to think. "Marie, have you eaten at The Waffle yet?"

It was surprisingly easy to get Marie's help, the woman was a sucker for a good waffle. Marie unlocked the door to the holding cells, allowing Sonja through.

"I didn't see anyone," the pink haired woman stated as she turned back to her desk.

Sonja headed through the doorway and into the room with the two small holding cells. It was a small town so they only used them occasionally for drunks and rambunctious tourists when they got into trouble. Maddy was the only one there, sitting in the far cell.

"Maddy?" she called.

The young girl quickly stood up. "Sonja? Is that you?"

"It's me," she answered, stepping close to the bars.

"Oh, I'm so glad to see you," the tired looking TV star exclaimed.

"What's going on? Why does Sheriff Thompson have you in here?"

"He thinks I'm the murderer, because of the note."

"I knew about the note, but that doesn't seem like enough evidence to hold you."

"I didn't write it," Maddy protested. "It looks like my handwriting but it's not."

"Is the note all he has on you?" Sonja asked.

The girl looked down at her feet. "No, it isn't," she whispered.

Sonja tilted her head, "What is it, Maddy?"

"The police found a heart shaped locket, my locket, on Spirit."

"Did you give him the locket?"

"No. I have no idea how he got it."

Sonja pieced a few things together. She remembered Maddy stroking Tech's sweaty hair while he lay in bed. "What was inside the locket?"

"A picture," Maddy said reluctantly.

"A picture of you and Tech together?"

Maddy's eyes widened in surprise. "How did you know?"

"I saw the way you looked at Tech last night. Were you secretly seeing Tech behind Spirit's back?"

Maddy nodded. "Spirit wasn't supposed to know. I was afraid of what he might do."

Sonja couldn't blame her for that. Spirit didn't seem like the most stable person she'd ever met.

"He found out because of the locket?"

"I didn't even know he had it," she admitted, "or how he got it."

The locket was just one more clue that placed Maddy at the scene of the crime. It also pointed toward a motive, that Maddy wanted Spirit out of the way so she could date Tech. If Spirit was abusive perhaps she thought killing him was her only way out of the relationship.

"But you didn't do it?" she asked, watching Maddy's expression closely.

"No," Maddy insisted.

"Okay, I have a favor to ask," Sonja commented. She reached into her purse and pulled out a small notepad she kept in there along with a pen. "Can you write a few words here and then sign your name?"

The young girl looked at her, confused.

"Just trust me," she urged.

Maddy took the pen and paper. "What should I write?"

"Anything, really."

Maddy went to work, scribbling on the paper. After a

moment, she handed it back. The paper said, "I did not kill Spirit," and it was signed, "Maddy."

"Thanks," Sonja said.

"What did you need that for?"

"I wanted to compare it to the handwriting I saw written on the letter." Sonja took a moment to examine the words, and more specifically the penmanship, carefully.

"And?" Maddy asked.

She nodded. "It doesn't look the same to me."

CHAPTER ELEVEN

As Sonja stepped out of the holding cell area, she caught sight of Sheriff Thompson escorting Benjamin out of the interrogation room. The cameraman caught sight of her and nodded a greeting.

Sheriff Thompson looked at Sonja with an eyebrow raised.

"Hi, Benjamin," she said, trying her hardest not to blush.

"Are you here to give your statement?" he asked.

She nodded.

"Well, I won't keep you then. Good to see you again." He turned toward Sheriff Thompson. "See ya, Sheriff."

Thompson raised a hand in farewell, his gaze still focused on Sonja.

Benjamin stepped out into the lobby.

"Sonja," the sheriff frowned, "what are you doing back here?"

She held up the notepad. "I was getting this," she replied.

"What is it?"

"I wanted to see Maddy's handwriting for myself. I watched her write this out and then looked at it. It looks like different handwriting to me."

"Look, Sonja. We have significant evidence against her now," he explained.

"I know," Sonja replied. "The locket."

The officer scowled.

Sonja shook her head. “I can’t stand by when an innocent girl might be convicted of a crime she didn’t commit.”

“That’s not your problem or responsibility. We have evidence that places her at the scene of the crime, we have a motive, and she had the means.”

“Have you sent the note along to be compared to her actual handwriting? To see if it matched?”

“I’m not going to discuss that with you, but even without the note, the locket places her at the scene of the crime.”

“What about all the other people on the farm that night? Have you even considered them?”

“Of course, we have, Sonja. Everyone else either has an alibi or simply has no apparent reason or motive.”

“And Benjamin?” Sonja felt her stomach sink even thinking of him as a murderer.

“We have no evidence at all that points to him.”

She sighed with relief. “There is just something I feel like we’re missing.”

"Well, it isn't your job to find out. It's mine. Go back to The Waffle. You're great at making food. Stick to that."

Sonja shoulders slumped, defeated. She was feeling beat at this point.

The sheriff placed a hand on her shoulder. "Come on, since you're here, let me get your statement at least."

She nodded.

"But after that, I don't want to see you until this case is closed."

Sonja followed him to the interrogation room.

After recounting the night's events for Sheriff Thompson, Sonja walked out to her car and got in. The sheriff seemed dead certain that Maddy was their culprit, and Sonja didn't have any good evidence to dispute the theory. She didn't even have any clue as to who the real murderer might be. Daniel Marston seemed the most likely, but—as the sheriff had mentioned multiple times—he had been locked up in the basement all evening.

Benjamin didn't have an alibi, but she couldn't see any real reason for him to commit the crime. She knew he wanted to quit show business but doubted it would create a strong enough motive to kill. And Mr. Hinkley was simply too old. He wouldn't have had the strength to lift a body up, but then again neither did Maddy.

Sonja was at a loss. She knew she needed something else. She needed evidence. There had to be something that she'd missed. She headed out of the parking lot, deciding she would make one more stop before going back home for the night. Ten minutes later she pulled into the parking lot of the Haunted Falls Hospital. It was a small tan building with only one floor and two wings, one for hospital rooms and one for testing, research, and exams.

"Hi," she said to the nurse at the admittance desk, "a young man came in this morning with a broken leg. I was wondering if you could tell me which room he's in?"

"Do you have any relation to the patient?"

Sonja hated to do it, but she knew that she had to lie. The hospital would never tell her which room was Tech's if she wasn't a relative.

"I'm his cousin," she smiled brightly, hoping that the receptionist didn't ask her for Tech's full name.

"Alright," the receptionist nodded toward the hallway on her right. "Go down to the very end -- it's the last room on your left."

"Thank you," Sonja replied, scurrying down the hall. She came to the open door and knocked.

"Come in," Tech called.

She stepped into the small room. Tech lay on his back in the hospital bed. His leg was in a cast and was elevated with a pulley system. "Hi," Sonja said, stepping in.

The young man looked up at her and smiled, confused. "Oh, hi. You're Sonja, right?

"Yes. Sonja Reed."

"And you helped me out last night."

She nodded.

"Thanks," he said. "I appreciate it."

"You looked like you were in pretty bad shape."

"I was," he admitted, "but I'm feeling comparatively better now."

"Well, I would hope so."

"Thanks, I heard you changed your mind about letting us film at the diner."

"I did, before the accident," she replied.

"The sooner we can get back to filming, the better."

That was odd. How could they go back to filming? Spirit was dead and Maddy was behind bars. "Is that even possible?"

"Yep, I think we should go on filming. I think it's what Spirit would want."

"And what about Maddy?" Sonja added. "She's currently a suspect in Spirit's murder."

The wounded TV star looked down, "I heard. The deputy told me when he came and got my statement. I'm hoping that she isn't actually the killer, but if she is, there is nothing I can do about it."

"And yet you want to go on filming?"

"Well, to stop now would be a crime, I think," he insisted. "You can't get a better story than this. A murder in association with one of the hauntings?"

This had nothing to do with honoring Spirit. It had to do with getting ratings, and if this went live it would make the ratings of the show potentially shoot through the roof.

"I was even thinking about maybe trying the barn again if Mr. Hinkley will allow us, and see if we can contact Spirit's spirit."

"I actually wanted to come in and talk to you about Spirit."

"What about him?"

"And about Maddy," she continued. "I don't think she committed this murder."

"Well, I hope not," Tech nodded. "But, it's not like we can change facts."

Sonja was astounded by how nonchalant he seemed about the situation.

"I would think you would be more worried about your girlfriend going to jail."

Tech's face went slightly pale. "How did you know that?"

"The police think she killed Spirit to get him out of the way so she could date you instead. They think she was afraid of him and didn't know what else to do. So, she killed him."

"That's crazy," Tech shook his head. "Our relationship had nothing to do with Spirit's death." This was the first sign of real emotion Tech had shown about the murder.

"That's not what the police believe," Sonja said, carefully watching his reaction. "They found a locket on the body. It had a picture of you and Maddy together in it."

"Well, if Maddy killed Spirit I had nothing to do with it," he protested.

"That much is obvious," she agreed. "How could you have been? You were upstairs in the bedroom with a broken leg." Sonja motioned to his cast.

Tech settled back. "Exactly."

"Of course, that doesn't mean you didn't help plan it," she prodded.

"I'd never do anything to hurt Spirit," he said matter-of-factly. "We've been best friends since elementary school."

"How long have you two known Maddy?"

"Only since college. Maddy started dating Spirit and the next thing we knew the three of us were filming videos together."

"I see."

"I suppose," he paused, "it could have been Maddy."

"What makes you say that?"

"Maddy wrote Spirit a note."

"You know about the note?" Sonja asked.

"Yes. She told me she was finished with him. She wanted to talk to him," he paused, "about us."

"Seems like poor timing."

"Maddy was never good with social cues. That's why she's 'The Mystic' in our group. She's better at dealing with ghosts than people."

Sonja would have to disagree on that front. Maddy seemed like the most amiable member of the group.

"So, did you see her leave to go to the barn?"

Tech thought for a minute. "No, I don't think so. I was pretty knocked out. I slept through most of the night."

"I think you were the only one who got any sleep," Sonja commented wryly. "You're sure you never woke up, didn't see or hear anything?"

"Not a peep."

The amateur sleuth sighed. She wasn't getting anywhere. All she had found was more evidence pointing toward Maddy as the killer.

"Well, I guess I'll let you rest," she remarked. "I'm sorry I bothered you."

"No problem," Tech replied.

Sonja turned to go and her purse caught on the bedside table. She stumbled, catching herself on the table. Tech's duffle bag went falling to the floor, spilling its contents everywhere. "Oh no. I'm so sorry." She could feel herself turning red with embarrassment.

"It's okay," he reassured her. "Accidents happen."

Sonja leaned down and started picking up the items and placing them back in the bag.

"It's just a bunch of junk anyway," he said.

Sonja put multiple things away, including the painkillers she remembered him taking the night before, and even the mud encrusted socks. "I haven't gotten a chance to wash them yet," Tech noted as she picked them up gingerly and placed them back in the bag.

Then she picked up something odd. There was a container of red, black, and purple eyeshadow in the bag.

What would he want with that? She held it up.

“Oh,” Tech exclaimed. “That’s Maddy’s.”

“Do you want me to take it to her?” she asked.

“No, that’s fine,” Tech replied. “Just put it in the bag, thanks.”

She placed it in the bag and put the bag back on the table.

“Thanks for coming.”

“No problem,” Sonja replied. “Get well soon.”

She turned and walked out of the room. Something told her that the container of eyeshadow didn’t belong to Maddy.

CHAPTER TWELVE

Sonja's head was spinning as she drove away. She felt like she was getting close to figuring things out. If she just had one more piece of the puzzle, maybe she could solve the case. She had her suspicions, they only needed to be validated.

Sonja drove directly back to the police station. She needed to talk to Sheriff Thompson again. As she parked the car, she spotted the deputies taking Daniel Marston up the steps of the station in handcuffs. She quickly got out. "What's going on here?"

"Police business," the deputies called back.

Sonja hurried into the building after them. To her surprise Maddy was standing at the front desk with Marie, signing papers. "What's happening?"

The young woman looked up and smiled. "They're letting me go."

"What? Why?" Sonja asked, eyeing Daniel as they dragged him into the back.

"They didn't say," she replied.

"Looks like they've got someone else in custody, hon," Marie added.

"I can see that," Sonja murmured.

Sheriff Thompson emerged from the back room. "Put him in cell two, boys."

Sonja quickly pushed toward him. "Sheriff?"

"You got it," one of the deputies replied.

"You can't do this," Daniel shouted in the officer's face. "You have no proof."

"Get him in there," Sheriff Thompson ordered.

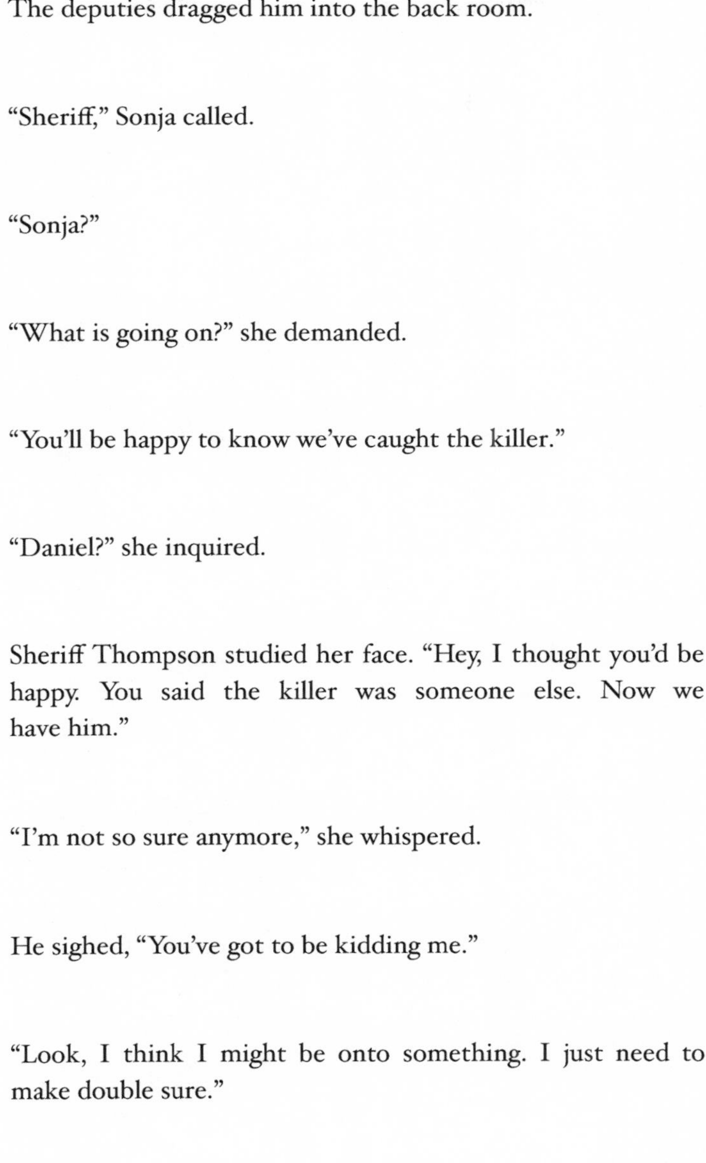

The deputies dragged him into the back room.

“Sheriff,” Sonja called.

“Sonja?”

“What is going on?” she demanded.

“You’ll be happy to know we’ve caught the killer.”

“Daniel?” she inquired.

Sheriff Thompson studied her face. “Hey, I thought you’d be happy. You said the killer was someone else. Now we have him.”

“I’m not so sure anymore,” she whispered.

He sighed, “You’ve got to be kidding me.”

“Look, I think I might be onto something. I just need to make double sure.”

"No, Sonja," he replied, "We have the guy we're after. Now let it go."

"Are you sure it's him," she insisted.

"Sonja, we're sure."

She sighed. "I'm sorry, Sheriff. I just don't see how it could be him. Wasn't he locked up all night long?"

"We thought so too, but new evidence shows otherwise. He had the means and definitely had the motive."

She supposed there may have been either a coal chute or a window well Daniel might have crawled out of, and if they had somehow found another piece of condemning evidence, either among Daniel's things or at the scene of the crime, then the case against him would be overwhelming.

"Now, as much as I appreciate your help," he remarked sarcastically, but teasingly, placing a hand on her shoulder, "I have a lot of paperwork to do." He squeezed her shoulder and then turned around and walked through the door.

Sonja stepped outside just as Maddy was heading down to the parking lot. "Maddy," she called.

The young woman turned around and waved. “Hi, Sonja. I’m walking back to the hotel.”

She hurried to catch up to her. “Let me give you a ride.”

“No thanks,” she said. “It’s a nice day. I prefer to walk.”

“Well, I’ll walk with you for a bit.”

“Thanks, I’ll enjoy the company.”

The pair started walking across the parking lot. “So, you don’t know why they let you out?”

“Not exactly. But I guess Daniel Marston is the murderer after all.”

Sonja sighed. “I’m not so sure.”

“They said I could go, and they were taking him in. Doesn’t that mean they have evidence against him?”

She nodded. “They do.”

"Then what's the problem?" Maddy asked.

"I feel like I'm missing something. That's all."

"Well, I wouldn't worry about it," she encouraged.

Sonja stopped, thinking as she stared into the distance.

"What is it?"

"Do you guys use makeup during your shoots?"

She nodded. "Of course, we do. That's normal for television—even reality television."

"Even the boys wear makeup?"

"Yes," she confirmed.

Sonja sighed. Her theory was out the window.

"What about purple or red eyeshadow?"

Maddy looked startled for a moment. "Purple or red eyeshadow? Where did you get that idea?"

"I visited Tech at the hospital today. He had purple and red eyeshadow in his bag."

"That's weird," she noted.

"He claimed it was yours."

"Mine?" The surprised TV star replied. "I would never wear purple or red eye shadow. It doesn't go well with my skin. Besides, it would look bad on camera."

"I guess that makes sense," she agreed. "I think I'm going to head back out to the farm."

Sonja walked toward her car.

"Why?" Maddy asked.

"I feel like I missed something." She knew it was right in front of her face. She just couldn't see it yet.

CHAPTER THIRTEEN

As Sonja pulled up to the farmhouse she noticed the van parked outside. “Oh no,” she whispered. “What now?”

She parked her car and got out. As she approached she could hear two voices talking inside the farmhouse through the screen door. She tiptoed up the steps and peeked in the open window. Benjamin and Mr. Hinkley were sitting at the table. Much to her surprise, both of them looked happy. She knocked on the door.

“Just a minute,” Mr. Hinkley called.

“I’ll get it,” Benjamin replied. Footsteps moved toward her and the door opened. There stood Benjamin. “Sonja, how are you?”

"Hello, Sonja," Mr. Hinkley called from the kitchen table. "Come in and have a cup of coffee with us."

She stared in confusion. "Come in," Benjamin instructed. "We were just having coffee."

"Uh, no thanks," she declined. "I just came out to see if the police had finished with their investigation out here."

The elderly farmer stood up from the table, leaning on his cane for support. "They have. Everything's cleared up. They've got the murderer."

"Yes, I heard that," she replied.

"And I have a new farm hand," Mr. Hinkley commented, beaming.

Sonja's jaw dropped, looking at Benjamin. "You?"

"Yep, it's me," he confirmed.

She could feel her heart hammering in her chest. "So, you're staying in Haunted Falls?"

"Yes. I'm finally getting out of show business."

Mr. Hinkley came and stood beside Benjamin in the doorway. "He's going to help me fix up the place, manage it."

"Oh?"

"Yep. After I finished talking to the sheriff today I got a call from the producer of The Spirit Show on the phone. Turns out, with the death of Spirit, they're going to be canceling the show mid-season. When I hung up I drove straight here. I apologized for everything that happened here last night, then I offered to help out on the farm in exchange for room and board."

Sonja was shocked. This was something she would have never expected, Mr. Hinkley allowing a stranger to stay on his land and help out with the farm. It seemed impossible.

"You must have made quite an impression in order to work that deal," she observed.

"Hogwash," the old farmer protested. "I need the help, and honestly, I've enjoyed talking to Benjamin. It will be a welcome change of pace to have some company out here with me." He smiled at the tall young man.

"Well, I'd better actually get things sorted out," Benjamin sighed, running a hand through his hair. "There's equipment that needs to be returned, and paperwork that I need to finish. I can't settle in as quickly as I'd like."

"Well, I'll look forward to seeing you again," the farmer shook his hand.

Benjamin walked down the steps toward the van.

"Mr. Hinkley, I'm surprised. What made you decide to let him stay here?" Sonja asked.

"Sonja," he muttered, holding his head down, "I owe you an apology."

"If anyone needs to apologize, it's me," she retorted.

"No, I was stubborn. I've been so lonely since Marjorie passed. I've let my loneliness make me sour. I've become a bitter old man." He hung his head and poked his cane at the floor. "I only wanted to be left alone."

"I know. I invaded your privacy just as much as the Spirit Crew did."

"Well, I realized, despite the chaos, that it was nice having people out on the farm again. There was life here again. So, when Benjamin came to apologize and asked to work as a farmhand, I immediately accepted his offer."

She smiled. "I'm thrilled things have worked out," she remarked.

For more reasons than one. She leaned down and gave Mr. Hinkley a hug. "Thank you."

She turned and headed down the steps, just as Benjamin was coming back up. "I think I forgot something in the study this morning."

"Oh, before you go," Mr. Hinkley asked, "has either of you seen a long black rope? It usually hangs on the wall in the barn. I can't seem to find it."

"Actually," the young cameraman replied, "I saw it upstairs in the guest bedroom last night."

Suddenly, Sonja remembered seeing it too. It had been sitting on the cane back chair in the corner of the room.

"What is it doing up there?" Mr. Hinkley asked. "Well, you can't always account for old age I suppose."

"I'll go get it for you," Benjamin offered.

"Let me come with you," Sonja insisted. They walked up the stairs to the guest bedroom. Sure enough, there was the black rope coiled on the chair.

"Got it," he declared picking it up.

Sonja paused, looking around the room. Suddenly, things started coming together in her mind. I've got it, she thought.

"Is something wrong, Sonja?"

"Do you have any paperwork? Files or forms that members of the Spirit Crew filled out?"

"Well, sure," he shrugged, "but why?"

"I just need to see some right away. It's very important."

"Alright," he remarked. "Follow me."

They rushed down the steps and handed the rope to Mr. Hinkley. "Why, it's all muddy and dirty," he complained.

"Come on," Sonja urged Benjamin on. "The paperwork."

"It's in the van," he commented, leading the way out the door.

They got to the van and opened the back doors. He reached in and pulled out a ragged looking folder. "Sorry, it's not in better condition."

"It doesn't matter," she dismissed. "As long as I can read them." She opened the file and flipped through a few pages. She stopped on one paper. She examined it closely. "This is it," she proclaimed.

"What is it?" he asked.

"I have a hunch, but I need your help with something," she remarked. "Can you hold onto that film equipment for one more day?"

CHAPTER FOURTEEN

Later that night, when it had just reached full dark, the remaining members of the Spirit Crew got together at Mr. Hinkley's barn to film one last farewell episode. Maddy pushed Tech up to the barn in the wheelchair.

"I can't believe you got Mr. Hinkley's permission for us to do this," she said to Sonja.

"I told him how important it was," she replied with a smile.

"It only seemed fitting as a final episode of the show, contacting the murdered spirit of one of our very own team members," Tech remarked excitedly.

"And he agreed that you guys could film it," Sonja replied, "so long as I was present to supervise the entire shoot."

"I couldn't be more grateful," Tech remarked. "This will be our most exciting episode yet, and maybe it will help the producer reconsider keeping the show on if he can see me and Maddy in action, on our own, without Spirit."

Maddy rubbed Tech's shoulders eagerly, both of them smiling.

"Alright," Sonja commented, "should we get started?"

Everyone nodded.

Benjamin brought the camera up, turned on the light, and indicated with a wave that he was recording.

"Welcome ghost hunters," Tech declared to the camera. "Tonight, we bring you a very special episode of The Spirit Show, potentially the most important ghost hunt in our entire career. Tonight, we visit the haunted barn on Hinkley Farm here in Haunted Falls—a town with a very dark history."

Sonja resisted the urge to roll her eyes. Tech was all cheese already, and they hadn't even gotten into the barn yet.

"This barn is the site of multiple horrible events. First, a rapist and a murderer hung himself in this barn after being overcome with guilt over his crimes. Secondly, I was attacked and wounded by an evil spirit the last time we were in here."

This time, she really did roll her eyes.

"And third," the ham of a TV host continued, "our very own Spirit—whom we loved dearly—was murdered in this barn, hung by the rafters in the same manner as the murderer from many years ago."

Maddy pushed the wheelchair closer to the front door of the barn.

"Tonight, we are trying to reach Spirit. We're seeking to speak with him one last time. If he speaks to us tonight, we'll know for sure that he has made it to the Other Side." He looked to Maddy, then to Sonja. "Tonight, we are accompanied by local diner owner, Sonja Reed."

Sonja nodded to the camera.

"She was the person who found Spirit's body. Hopefully, her presence will help bring his spirit forth. Now, we'll head inside the barn."

He nodded at Sonja who opened the large barn door. Maddy rolled him inside and Sonja and Benjamin followed.

"Here we are inside the barn," Tech commented. "Mystic," he called, looking at Maddy, "do you sense any presence here?"

Maddy closed her eyes, stretched out her hands, and moved around the room. "I do," she whispered. "I do sense some sort of energy here in the room."

"Alright," Tech replied. "We have a confirmation that there is a definite energy in the room. Now let's see what we can pick up on the Seer." He slipped the device out of its pouch and lifted it, looking around the room. "If there truly is an entity or spirit here, hopefully, we can catch a glimpse of it."

There was the sudden sound of quiet whispers on the air.

"Do you hear that?" Maddy observed. "I can hear them trying to speak to us."

"Turn me that way," Tech instructed, pointing toward the beam where Spirit had been hung. He held up the Seer, looking directly into the device's screen. "I think we're getting something here."

Tech squinted and pulled the Seer close to his face.

There was a sudden bang, followed by a sickening snap. Tech's eyes grew wide. He shouted, dropping the Seer in the dirt.

"What is it?" Maddy asked. "What did you see?"

Tech's face had gone pale. "I-I saw a face in the Seer. Coming toward me."

"Was it Spirit? Was it Spirit's face?"

He looked up, "It was." He turned to look at the camera. He was visibly shaking. "This beam here, where I just witnessed the face coming toward me in the Seer, is where Spirit's body was found."

"I can feel his presence," Maddy added. "It's incredibly strong."

"Speak to him, Mystic. Speak to him," Tech cried.

"Spirit," Maddy yelled out. "If you are truly here, if you can hear me, speak to us."

A voice rang out through the barn. I'm heeeeere.

“That’s him,” Maddy declared, her eyes brimming with excitement.

Tech was shaking uncontrollably now. “It’s him? It’s really him?” He whispered.

I know what you did . . . the voice echoed.

“Stop it. Stop that voice,” Tech cried. “It’s not Spirit. It can’t be Spirit.”

You won’t get awaaaay . . . the voice went on.

“No, no, no.” The frightened TV host looked all around the room and pushed his wheelchair backward.

“What are you doing?” Maddy whispered.

“No, it’s a trick,” he cried. “It’s not real.”

“Tech. Calm down,” she pleaded.

He pushed his wheelchair back further, turning, trying to see the entire room at once. He pushed the chair until he was directly under the beam where the body had hung.

"You're not real," he shouted.

Then, everyone gasped. Tech screamed.

A blue shadowy figure dropped down like a rock, right in front of Tech, and hung there from an invisible cord. The figure's eyes bulged out and looked directly at Tech.

Sonja felt her heart hammer in her chest as she stared through the translucent figure.

"No, no," he screamed. "Leave me alone. I killed you. You're dead, Spirit. You're dead."

Instantly, light flooded the room. Tech blinked, and looked up. The figure was gone.

Sonja stood near a large flood light. "That's all we needed."

Tech looked over at Sonja. "What? What's going on?"

"You just admitted to the murder of Spirit."

"I-I don't understand," Tech muttered.

"We rigged the place," she responded. "We had sound effects and other special effects set up to scare you into confessing. Benjamin helped me."

"But, I heard his voice."

"We used sound bites from old clips," Benjamin replied. "I just remixed them to say the right thing, and to sound spooky of course."

"And everything we filmed is going directly to the police and to Sheriff Thompson."

"That-that's not possible," Tech tried to argue. "I couldn't have killed Spirit. I was up in the guest bedroom the whole time. My leg is broken."

"No," Sonja retorted. "Your leg wasn't broken. Not yet, anyway."

His face twisted in fear. "No. It's not true."

"I'm afraid so," she confirmed. "I didn't figure it out until I realized why you had that makeup in your bag. You see, it all started in the barn when Daniel pretended to break your leg. Sheriff Thompson was partially right. Daniel was in on the murder. Daniel himself told us that he is a professional trainer for stuntmen. He would know exactly how to kick your leg and make it look real, real enough for all of us to believe it had actually happened. After that, Maddy and Spirit carried you into the house, and while they were carrying you, you slipped the note and the locket into Spirit's pocket. That way he wouldn't know where the note had actually come from and would only assume it was from Maddy.

"Once inside the farmhouse you insisted on both having your bag—for your pain pills you said—and on using the bathroom. So, we helped you into the bathroom and gave you your duffle bag. Once the bathroom door was securely shut, you did a quick makeup job on your leg to make it look severely bruised. Then we brought you back to the bed and did some quick first aid on what we thought was a broken leg, but that wasn't the case.

"Once everyone had dispersed, me to the master bedroom, Maddy into the bathroom for a shower, and Spirit out to the barn—just as the note you gave him instructed—you got up from the bed. Then, using the rope you had stolen from the barn and slipped into the duffle bag, you climbed down and went out to the barn yourself.

"We had already taken off your boots, and you didn't want to risk taking the time to slip them on, so you went out in just your socks. That's why your socks were so wet and muddy when they shouldn't have been. Once you got to the barn, you snuck up behind Spirit, slipped the electrical cord around his neck and hoisted him up on the beam. When you were sure he was dead, you ran back to the house, climbed up the rope into the bedroom, and then using something for leverage—the cane chair perhaps—you broke your own leg for real. You got back in the bed, truly in pain this time, and waited for someone to return and find you."

Tech hung his head in shame, still shaking from adrenalin. "He deserved it. Daniel and I hated Spirit. He threatened to kick me and Maddy off the show. This show was my life," he whispered,

"He was threatening to take it all away from me. I knew he could do it, too. The producers loved him. He was the whole reason they picked us up in the first place. So, I knew I had to get rid of him. That way the show would become mine, and with his death, the ratings would shoot through the roof." Tech buried his head in his hands and Maddy cried silently.

"Too bad the show just got canceled instead," Benjamin remarked, shaking his head in disgust.

"I had a strange feeling at the hospital," Sonja nodded. "Your nonchalant attitude toward Spirit's death, and more importantly toward Maddy being the main suspect, clued me in. You didn't care if Maddy took the blame, as long as you didn't get caught, but once I saw the makeup, I got very curious. I was confused about why you would have that style of makeup in your bag, but when I saw the muddy rope in the room upstairs, everything started coming together."

"I asked Benjamin to show me some paperwork, so that I could see a sample of your handwriting. When I saw it, I knew it was you who wrote the note to Spirit, not Maddy."

Tech began to cry. "It was a perfect plan. Everything would have been mine."

Sonja stared at him, unmoved. "Your greed was your downfall, and now you've lost everything."

"Couldn't happen to a nicer guy," Benjamin muttered, arms crossed.

CHAPTER FIFTEEN

Sheriff Thompson arrived a few minutes later and took Tech away in handcuffs, loading him into the back of the police cruiser.

"Well, it looks like you were right," he admitted.

Sonja nodded, "I'm sorry for sticking my nose where it doesn't belong."

"Well, thankfully we now have both suspects in custody."

"I'm glad to help where I can."

"Next time, let me handle it," he instructed. "Got it?"

"Got it," she agreed.

Sheriff Thompson squeezed her shoulder and got in the cruiser and headed for the police station.

Maddy stood by, dazed and crying.

Sonja placed a hand on her shoulder. "I'm so sorry."

Maddy wiped the tears from her cheeks.

"I just wasn't expecting this," she said softly. "Tech always seemed so kind. He was the most level-headed person on our team."

"I know this must be painful," Sonja sympathized. "What will you do now?"

Maddy shrugged, miserable. "The show is over, both Spirit and Tech are gone. Benjamin is staying here. I suppose I'll just return home. I haven't seen my mom and dad in probably three years."

"That sounds like a good plan," Sonja tried to be encouraging.

Maddy nodded. "After all this chaos I think it will be good to see them." She picked something up from a pile of equipment. "Here, I want you to have this." She held out the pouch with the Seer inside.

"You want me to have it? Don't you need to return it to the studio?"

She shook her head. "Spirit built it himself, but now I feel like it belongs to you."

"I couldn't take it," she admitted.

"I want you to. I want you to be able to remember us," Maddy smiled faintly. "Well, remember me."

She nodded. "Alright. I'm sure I'd never forget you with or without it, but I'll take it," she agreed, thinking that Sheriff Thompson might want it for evidence.

Maddy held the pouch out and Sonja took it.

"Well," she sighed, "I guess I'll be seeing you."

Sonja nodded. "Bye. Take care."

Maddy opened the passenger door on the van and slid in.

"Looks like we're off," Benjamin commented, walking up to the van and closing Maddy's door for her.

"Your flight back to L.A. is tomorrow morning?" Sonja asked, when he came back around to the driver's side.

"Early," he replied. "We'll need to be out of here at around 5:30 to be to the airport on time."

"When do you think you'll be back in Haunted Falls?" Sonja asked.

"I shouldn't be gone more than a week or two. I'm just dropping off equipment and then moving out of my apartment. I'll probably need to sell some stuff as well."

"Well, I'll be looking for you when you come back," she grinned, biting her lip shyly. "Come into the diner and I'll give you a free plate of waffles. With bacon."

"Thanks, I appreciate that," Benjamin's smile was warm.

"And you'll make sure Maddy gets home okay?"

"Yeah," he confirmed, loading a few last items into the back of the van. "I'll look after her, make sure she gets back to her mom and dad."

"Good."

Benjamin came back around to the driver's side. "You know, there's still one thing that I don't quite understand," he admitted.

"What's that?"

"How did you get the ghostly figure of Spirit to appear over Tech? I didn't set that up. I don't even have the equipment to do something like that."

Sonja shook her head. "I didn't set that up."

"Then who did?"

She shivered. "I think it's safe to say Spirit set it up himself."

A SNEAK PEEK

Sinister Strawberry Waffle

Diner of the Dead, Book 3

Prologue

Bill Merrill had just finished filling out the last dregs of the day's paperwork when the phone rang. Debating whether he should answer the call or not, he stared at the phone. It was, after all, already past six, and the office at Merrill and Macklin's Landscapes and More had technically been closed for over an hour.

The phone continued to ring.

I'll just let it go to voice mail, the business owner decided. It had already been a long, hard day, and his only wish now was to head home, eat dinner, and fall asleep in front of the TV.

Grabbing the manila folder off the desk, he walked across the small mobile office to the filing cabinet. The double wide trailer made for a small work space overall but was sufficient for the company's needs. This setup also made it easier to remain stationed next to the storage warehouse where Merrill kept all the equipment, tools, and gardening supplies he used in his business.

The phone finally stopped ringing, beeped, and then transferred to the answering machine. The sound of Merrill's voice echoed back from the machine. "You've reached Merrill and Macklin's Landscapes and More. Neither Merrill nor Macklin are available to take your call at the moment. Please leave your name, number, and a short message and we will get back to you as soon as possible. Thank you for your patronage."

Merrill laughed a little at himself. The answering machine sounded overly professional and formal—nothing like he actually felt or acted in real life.

The phone beeped again and then the message began. He paused to listen.

At first, there seemed to be no one on the line—just empty silence.

He expected the line to click and whoever it was to call back another day.

Then, noticing the faint labored breathing, he realized the person on the other end sounded tired, labored—sick even.

Dashing for the phone Merrill almost answered it, but the voice on the line cut him off before he could get there.

"Bill . . . Merrill . . ." the voice strained. "Do not . . . sign the contract . . . for The Waffle diner."

The landscaper's face, worn with deep lines from age, twisted in confusion. "What?"

"Do not . . . sign . . . with Sonja Reed."

Stomping across the office, Merrill threw the file in his hand down on the desk.

With a clean swipe, he picked up the phone from its cradle. "Who is this?"

The line went dead and Merrill looked at the phone in his hand. Don't sign the contract for The Waffle diner? Why not? Sonja Reed was one of the nicest and most upstanding young women Merrill had the privilege of knowing. She deserved his services just as much as any other person in Haunted Falls. He replaced the phone in its cradle.

Looking at the file he'd tossed on the desk, where it had fallen open, he read the paper on top. It was a contract, the one he had just finished filling out before the phone call came in—it was made out to Sonja Reed, owner of The Waffle diner.

Chapter 1

The Colorado mountainside was dressed in a thick shroud of fog, the trees nothing more than blank, darkened figures standing among the gray light. All details of the normally green foliage appeared washed out, as if filtered through a poor quality camera lens.

Wandering, bewildered, her bare feet sinking into the cold soft earth, Sonja shivered in her white tank top and yellow plaid sleep shorts. A low breeze brushed the exposed skin, and the frigid mountain air prickled against her arms and legs.

"Hello?" she called, stumbling along. Her voice seemed to catch in the heavy fog and stop dead in the air.

A drop of rain touched her bare shoulder, running down her arm until it dropped off into the dirt.

"Oh, no," she whispered.

The rain came on quickly, coating the trees and earth in a wet sheen. Running now, Sonja desperately tried to find shelter. She couldn't remember how she'd gotten out here, and had no idea where she was. Face twisted in worry, and clothes already beginning to soak through, she darted back and forth between the rocks and trees searching for some sign of life, for the light of a building.

Her feet began to sink further into the wet earth with each fresh step. Mud caked onto the soles of her feet, hanging there as clumps, before sliding off again and plopping to the ground.

"Hello?" she bleated again, feeling helpless.

Shivering uncontrollably now, she pushed onward. Her soaked clothes clung to her skin, enveloping her in a damp cold which seeped right down into her bones. A faint noise caught her attention, barely audible above the heavy rainfall. It sounded like fresh earth scraping against metal.

"Hello?" she inquired a third time, stepping into a small clearing.

The figure of a man was bent down, his legs partially hidden in the ground, as he shoveled piles of heavy, wet dirt up and out of a deep hole. A thick brown coat was wrapped tight around his body, the collar pulled up over his neck. A ratty baseball cap obscured his face.

"Excuse me? I need help," she murmured tentatively, stepping close to the hole.

Stopping dead in her tracks Sonja felt the cold reach her heart, piercing it like an icy dagger. There was a woman in the hole, all pale skin and muddy hair. Sonja knew instantly that she was dead. Heart thundering, she backed away from the hole. The grave digger turned slowly to look at her. The brim of the ball cap moved upward revealing his face.

Sonja's mouth went dry and her throat hoarse. "D-Dad?"

Her father smiled wickedly. A blood-curdling shriek erupted from the hole, breaking through the gentle hum of the rain. The pale corpse sat up in its grave, its claw-like hands grabbing the man by the coat. Screaming like a child, the undead corpse's grip firm on his lapels, her father slowly began to sink down into the ground.

"Dad!" Sonja cried.

Her eyes widening in fright, she reached out a hand and tried to tear her father from the woman's grasp, but it was no use. Before her very eyes he slipped through her fingers and sunk into the muddy earth, disappearing into its wet abyss.

***

Sitting bolt upright in bed, Sonja realized she was at home. Her whole body shivered and her skin glistened with a sheen of cold sweat. The window near her bed stood open, the cool mountain breeze wafting in and chilling her damp skin. Another nightmare. Ever since she returned to her hometown of Haunted Falls, she had been having them, and they seemed to be getting worse. Leaning forward, she rested her head in her hands.

While unpleasant, the nightmares were entirely understandable. Since moving back to the small mountain town, Sonja had been involved as a witness in two harrowing murder cases. Worse than that, she had experienced several terrifying encounters that one could only explain as being of the "supernatural" variety. Skeptical at first, she was quickly beginning to believe that ghosts truly did exist—a strange fact she wished she could forget.

The one thing Sonja didn't understand was why her absent father continually appeared in her nightmares. She had seen him only once in the last four years, just a few weeks earlier. He came and went like the wind without an explanation of why he had abandoned her and her mother, or where he was going.

Standing up from her bed, the shadow of many restless nights under her eyes, Sonja moved across the room, knowing that she wouldn't be getting back to sleep tonight. Flipping the switch on the coffee pot first, she headed to her antique oak desk, powered on her computer and opened the Word document that held her unfinished book manuscript. The dreams that she had left behind in New York when she returned home to Haunted Falls still beckoned to her, taunted her. She may never see anything that she wrote get to a bestseller list, but she still yearned to give her dream a try. The frustrated but tenacious writer decided she would escape into a world of her own making, and write until the morning sunlight chased the remaining shreds of darkness from the sky.

ALSO BY CAROLYN Q. HUNTER

Diner of the Dead Series

Book 1: The Wicked Waffle

Book 2: Battered and Buttered Waffle

Book 3: Sinister Strawberry Waffle

Book 4: The Wayward Waffle

Book 5: Pumpkin Pie Waffle

Book 6: Turkey and Terror

Book 7: Creepy Christmas Waffle

Book 8: Birthday Cake Waffle

Book 9: Spooky Sweetheart Waffle

Book 10: Eerie Irish Waffle

Book 11: Savory Spring Waffle

Book 12: Benedict Waffle

Book 13: Scary Sausage Waffle

Book 14: Murderous Mocha Waffle

Book 15: Red Velvet Waffle

Book 16: High Steaks Murder

Book 17: Hole In One Waffle

Book 18: Fireworks and Waffles

Book 19: Games, Ghouls and Waffles

Book 20: Waffling in Murder

The Wicked Waffle Series

Book 1:Hot Buttered Murder

Book 2: Bacon Caramel Murder

Book 3: Thanksgiving Waffle Murder

Book 4: Christmas Waffle Caper

Book 5: Buckaroo Waffle Murder

Book 6: Wedding Waffle Murder

Book 7: Cactus Waffle Murder

Book 8: Zombie Waffle Murder

Book 9: A Very Catty Murder

Book 10: Halloween Waffle Murder

Pies and Pages Series

Book 1: Killer Apple Pie

Book 2: Killer Chocolate Pie

Book 3: Killer Halloween Pie

Book 4: Killer Thanksgiving Pie

Book 5: Killer Christmas Pie

Book 6: Killer Caramel Pie

Book 7: Killer Cocoa Pie

Book 8: Shamrock Pie Murder

Book 9: Killer Easter Pie

Book 10: Killer Cheesecake Tart

Book 11: Summer Smore Murder

Book 12: Maple Nut Murder

Book 13: Tea, Thyme, and Murder

Book 14: A Harvest of Murder

Book 15: Perfectly Pumpkin Killer

Book 16: Killer Acorn Pie

Book 17: Killer Chocolate Pecan Pie

Dead-End Drive-In Series

Book 1: Sisterly Screams

Book 2: Moans, Mummies and Murder

Book 3: Blue Eyed Doll

Book 4: Movies and Murder

The Cracked Mirror Series

Book 1: The Biker and The Boogeyman

Holiday Standalones

Hooked on Holidays

Moored in Murder

AUTHOR'S NOTE

I'd love to hear your thoughts on my books, the storylines, and anything else that you'd like to comment on—reader feedback is very important to me. My contact information, along with some other helpful links, is listed on the next page. If you'd like to be on my list of "folks to contact" with updates, release and sales notifications, etc.... just shoot me an email and let me know. Thanks for reading!

Also...

... if you're looking for more great reads, Summer Prescott Books publishes several popular series by outstanding Cozy Mystery authors.

CONTACT SUMMER PRESCOTT BOOKS PUBLISHING

Twitter: @summerprescott1

Bookbub: https://www.bookbub.com/authors/summer-prescott

Blog and Book Catalog: http://summerprescottbooks.com

Email: summer.prescott.cozies@gmail.com

YouTube: https://www.youtube.com/channel/UCngKNUkDdWuQ5k7-Vkfrp6A

And...be sure to check out the Summer Prescott Cozy Mysteries fan page and Summer Prescott Books Publishing Page on Facebook – let's be friends!

To download a free book, and sign up for our fun and exciting newsletter, which will give you opportunities to win prizes and swag, enter contests, and be the first to know about New Releases, click here: http://summerprescottbooks.com

Made in the USA
Columbia, SC
27 October 2023